CRANFORD PUBLIC LIBRARY N.J.
3 9520 00136 8549

O9-BRZ-150

The New Lieutenant

BY THE SAME AUTHOR

Whistle and I'll Come
The Kid
Storm South
Hopkinson and the Devil of Hate
Leave the Dead Behind Us
Marley's Empire
Bowering's Breakwater
Sladd's Evil
A Time for Survival
Poulter's Passage
The Day of the Coastwatch
Man, Let's Go On
Half a Bag of Stringer
The German Helmet
The Oil Bastards
Pull My String
Coach North
Flood
The Last Farewell
A Lady of the Line
Kidnap

Featuring SIMON SHARD
Call for Simon Shard
A Very Big Bang
Blood Run East
The Eros Affair
Blackmail North
Shard Calls the Tune
The Hoof
Shard at Bay
The Executioners
Overnight Express
The Logan File
The Abbot of Stockbridge

Featuring LIEUTENANT ST VINCENT HALFHYDE, RN
Beware, Beware the Bight of Benin
Halfhyde's Island
The Guns of Arrest
Halfhyde to the Narrows
Halfhyde for the Queen
Halfhyde Ordered South
Halfhyde and the Flag Captain
Halfhyde on the Yangtze
Halfhyde on Zanatu
Halfhyde Outward Bound
The Halfhyde Line
Halfhyde and the Chain Gangs
Halfhyde Goes to War
Halfhyde on the Amazon
Halfhyde and the Admiral
Halfhyde and the Fleet Review

Featuring DONALD CAMERON, RNVR:
Cameron, Ordinary Seaman
Cameron Comes Through
Cameron of the Castle Bay
Lieutenant Cameron, RNVR
Cameron's Convoy
Cameron in the Gap
Orders for Cameron
Cameron in Command
Cameron and the Kaiserhof
Cameron's Raid
Cameron's Chase
Cameron's Troop Lift
Cameron's Commitment
Cameron's Crossing

Featuring COMMANDER SHAW
Gibraltar Road
Redcap
Bluebolt One
The Man from Moscow
Warmaster
Moscow Coach
The Dead Line
Skyprobe
The Screaming Dead Balloons
The Bright Red Businessmen
The All-Purpose Bodies
Hartinger's Mouse
This Drakotny . . .
Sunstrike
Corpse
Werewolf
Rollerball
Greenfly
The Boy Who Liked Monsters
The Spatchcock Plan
Polecat Brennan
Burn-Out

Featuring COMMODORE JOHN MASON KEMP, RD, RNR
The Convoy Commodore
Convoy North
Convoy South
Convoy East
Convoy of Fear
Convoy Homeward

Featuring TOM CHATTO
Apprentice to the Sea
The Second Mate

Nonfiction
Tall Ships: The Golden Age of Sail
Great Yachts

The New Lieutenant

PHILIP McCUTCHAN

St. Martin's Press
New York

 For information, address St. Martin's Press, 175 Fifth Avenue, New York, N.Y. 10010.

Library of Congress Cataloging-in-Publication Data

McCutchan, Philip.
The new lieutenant / Philip McCutchan.
p. cm.
ISBN 0-312-15604-9
I. Title.
PR6063.A167N48 1997
823'.914—dc21 97-10026
CIP

First published in Great Britain by
George Weidenfeld & Nicolson Ltd.

First U.S. Edition: July 1997

10 9 8 7 6 5 4 3 2 1

To my granddaughters: in order of seniority
Alice, Grace and Mary McCutchan and Joanna Speer,
with much love.

AUTHOR'S NOTE

Although Tom Chatto is not himself derived from any particular person, parts of this book are based broadly upon an interview with my father, Captain Donald Robert McCutchan, in the *Toronto Star* newspaper of 2 July 1932. In 1914 my father was Second Officer of the Pacific Steam Navigation Company's R.M.S. *Ortega,* homeward bound under Captain Douglas Reid Kinnear from Valparaiso round Cape Horn, when the liner was fired upon by the German cruiser *Dresden,* north of the Magellan Strait; and it was my father who led the ship, by taking soundings from a seaboat, through uncharted waters to Punta Arenas. On arrival back in the UK, he joined the Royal Naval Reserve and served largely in Q ships thereafter.

The New Lieutenant

ONE

TOM CHATTO, AS THE YEARS OF RUNning between Liverpool and Valparaiso went past, had begun to feel a restlessness. Not against the sea; far from that. He was a dedicated seaman with expectations of one day getting his own command as Master of a liner. But there was the restlessness brought on by the familiarity of the run, despite the ever-changing weather conditions, the blazing sun often enough in the South Atlantic, the gales and high seas as the ship dropped south between the Falkland Islands and the Argentinian coast, the ice and westerlies off the pitch of the Horn. Despite, also, the large variety of passengers carried on each voyage out and home.

Boredom? Not quite that. There was plenty to occupy the mind of a watchkeeping officer on the bridge at sea . . .

In any event a change was coming, and had been seen in the offing a year or so past as relations worsened between King George and his cousin the German Emperor. The lives of all who went to sea were to be changed beyond recognition.

On a grey, sea-disturbed day in that early August of 1914 the main fleets of the British Navy had been stationary in their review lines in Spithead off Portsmouth, premier port of the Empire, ships manned fore and aft with sennit-hatted seamen, to salute the King-Emperor, His Majesty King George V, as he passed by aboard the Royal Yacht *Victoria and Albert*. But this was to be no ordinary review such as was customarily held in honour of coronations and royal anniversaries. That day, as the sun went down towards the great jags of the Needles rocks on the Isle of Wight, and the long lines of battleships, battle-cruisers, armoured and light cruisers, destroyers and submarines faded into the gloom past St Catherine's Point, they were already steaming to their war stations. Although at the time no one could make a forecast, the ships would not resume their peace-time activities for the next four long years, by which time they would have steamed through many thousands of miles of war-torn seas to engage the enemy above and below the surface.

For some while the storms of war had been gathering; Sir Edward Grey, His Majesty's Secretary of State for Foreign Affairs, had told a Foreign-Office audience that the lamps were going out all over Europe, and would not be lit again in his time.

In the naval town of Portsmouth the faces were not so grim; there was almost an air of celebration. It was high time the sabre-rattling Kaiser Wilhelm, and Little Willy his strutting son, were taught a lesson they would never forget. The seamen of the British Navy welcomed war; it was what they had been trained for. Already the men of the Royal Fleet Reserve, petty officers and sailors whose time of active service had expired, had been called out by Royal proclamation. And recruiting of the Hostilities Only men had started. As Their Majesties King George and Queen Mary left from the harbour railway station in the royal train for Waterloo, a bluejacket band marched ahead of a company of seamen with rifles and bayonets fixed, playing patriotic songs from the days of the South African war: 'Goodbye Dolly Gray' and 'Soldiers of the Queen'; also the song that was to be sung so often in the bloody mud of the Flanders trenches: 'It's a long way to Tipperary' . . .

In Liverpool on the Mersey, as the Pacific Steam Navigation Company's liner *Orsino* prepared to sail once again for the River Plate and Valparaiso in Chile round Cape Horn, it was much the same. From Carlisle Castle had come the fifes and drums of the 1st Battalion The Border Regiment to join The King's Liverpool Regiment, whose depot brass led the parade along Lime Street down to the landing stage where a troop transport stood ready to embark for France. Union flags, and the Red Ensign of the Merchant Service upon whose ships and seamen the prosperity of the port of Liverpool depended, waved in their thousands along the route and the marching soldiers were cheered every foot of the way. Among those watching from the decks of the merchant vessels in the river was Tom Chatto, standing with Captain Fullbright on the bridge of the *Orsino*, to which ship he had transferred, with Captain Fullbright at the latter's request to the Company, from the *Orvega*. There was a strange stirring in his guts as he listened to the brass, a stirring that increased as the wires and ropes of the troopship were cast off and the last gangway brought ashore, and the combined fifes and drums of the two battalions, formed up on the landing stage, played the soldiers out to the strains of 'Auld Lang Syne'.

War. At this early stage the thoughts were of glory, honour, conquest, all mixed with a kind of nostalgia and a desire to be part of it all. The disillusion would come later, with the lengthening casualty lists, the sinkings, the zeppelin raids over England.

But not yet . . .

As next day the *Orsino* took her place at the landing stage to embark her outward-bound passengers, and then as the liner moved off the quay to head for the Skerries and the turn south for St George's Channel, Tom wondered what changes he would find in Liverpool when the ship returned across the seas of war. In the lead-in to the war situation there had been talk in maritime circles of many things, among them the possibility of using camouflage paint as some protection against enemy surface ships, commerce raiders, and the threat posed by the German U-boats, the *Unterzeebooten* that would wage an alien kind of warfare against unarmed merchant ships, against women and children aboard the liners and against the flow of urgently needed imports. It was well enough known that Britain depended upon her merchant shipping to bring in the supplies from overseas – the food, the oil, perhaps the munitions that might be supplied by the United States if President Wilson could be persuaded by Mr Churchill, First Lord of the Admiralty. Camouflage would destroy the visible identity of the various shipping lines, their house colours, their individuality, and that alone would cause a visual change in the Mersey. But that was a small enough point, Tom thought. Liverpool would remain herself, physically untouched by war, though there would be much grieving in the years ahead for seamen lost at sea – if the war lasted for any length of time, that was, which was surely an impossibility. Great Britain had the world's strongest navy: effectively, some forty battleships, four battle-cruisers, one hundred and twenty cruisers of various sizes, two hundred and twenty torpedo-boat destroyers and seventy-three submarines. The German Emperor's navy could be no match for all that.

The liner proceeded that sailing day through peaceful seas, taking her departure from the Fastnet Rock off Cape Clear, with a full passenger list in all three classes, first, second and steerage. During the voyage – at least until an enemy-inspired delay in Montevideo – there was little talk of war. The dances, the boat-deck dalliances, the deck games and the sumptuous meals continued as ever they had done in peace-time. The war was going to be over by Christmas, ending in a glorious victory for the British Army and Navy, with the Kaiser grovelling at the feet of King George in Buckingham Palace.

Yet it was very obviously to be the liner's last peace-time voyage; and for Tom Chatto the homeward run would be his last in the ships of the PSNC, while the war continued. Before sailing from the Mersey he had investigated the possibility of entering the Royal Naval Reserve, to fight the war with guns and armour at his disposal. He had spoken to the Line about this; they had been understanding but dismayed.

'You have excellent prospects with the Line, Chatto,' the Marine Superintendent had said. 'I'm authorized by the Board to tell you this: you could be First Officer next voyage. After that a command wouldn't be so far ahead.' He'd shrugged. 'But if you've made up your mind . . . well, there's no more to be said. However, we'll expect you to talk to us again when the *Orsino* returns. Maybe you'll have had second thoughts, who knows?' But on arrival in Montevideo the ship was held in port for a matter of weeks on account of German commerce raiders being reported as waiting outside the Plate, to intercept and sink Allied vessels entering and leaving. Such interference with the PSNC schedule made Tom see red; and he knew that his mind was made up. He would join the war at sea in a fighting capacity.

A normal run, except for that irritating delay in Montevideo; but, on the liner's eventual arrival in Valparaiso, things began to change very sharply. By this time Britain had been at war for some weeks, and the *Orsino*'s routine homeward passenger embarkation had been interrupted. When the Line's agent came aboard to be closeted with Fullbright and the purser, it turned out that most of the normal bookings had been cancelled by order of the War Office in London. In Valparaiso there were some five hundred French citizens, all of them reservists of the French Army who had come in from all over Chile for transport home in order to rejoin the Colours and fight for France beleaguered by the German divisions pouring in through Belgium. What was left of the passenger accommodation would be allocated to British citizens wishing to return home with, in a number of cases, their wives and children. With the war moving into its stride, as it were, it would be a big responsibility for the Master. After the Montevideo experience, it was common knowledge that German surface ships were in the South Atlantic, possibly in the South Pacific as well, among them the light cruisers *Dresden*, *Nürnberg*, *Leipzig* and *Emden*, all of them carrying ten 4.1-inch guns in twin turrets and well armoured with protective plating.

The *Orsino* left Valparaiso in fairly apprehensive fashion. Fullbright reinforced the orders that had been issued initially when hostilities had been declared. To his heads of departments he stressed again the overridingly important points.

'No lights on the open decks after sunset – and that includes no smoking. All square ports to be blacked out, all ports to have the deadlights clamped down throughout the ship. In the event of trouble, all watertight doors will be shut immediately. Exercising boat drill and exercising the stewards' fire parties will be carried out daily and any deficiencies will be reported to me at once.'

All hands, and especially the lookouts at the foremasthead and in the bridge wings, were on full alert as the liner came out into the South Pacific to head down for the passage of Cape Horn.

The first alarm came as the liner was still north of the Pacific entry to the Magellan Strait, standing into weather that for the Cape Horn area was fair; and the visibility was good. There had been no sign of any other vessels ahead or on either beam, but when the report came from the foremasthead, Fullbright remembered what he had in fact never forgotten: those warships outside the Plate, the German East Asiatic Squadron under Vice-Admiral Graf von Spee.

The report was brief, uninformative to some extent: 'Smoke on the horizon, sir, dead ahead.'

The officers on *Orsino*'s bridge lifted their binoculars on to the bearing. Fullbright said, 'Gut reaction, Mr Chatto. I see only smoke. There may be nothing in it. Nevertheless, full precautions.'

Tom understood and acted fast, passing down the order

for the watertight doors to be closed, and the fire parties stood to their sections below. Fullbright himself spoke to the engine-room via the voice-pipe. 'Captain here. Unknown vessel ahead. Stand by for immediate alterations in revolutions – Chief Engineer to go to the starting-platform. Mr Chatto?'

'Sir?'

'Have the purser informed.' The purser would know the drill: all ship's papers and cash to be ready for jettisoning overboard in lead-weighted bags. Fullbright resumed his study of the ahead bearing. There was still just the smoke; the ship herself was hulldown, not even the funnels visible as yet. But within the next two minutes a little more emerged and once again the lookout reported from the foremasthead. 'Three funnels, sir. Three grey funnels . . . I reckon she's a warship, sir!'

Fullbright stiffened.

Then another report: 'German ensign, sir! I reckon she's the *Dresden*, sir.'

Fullbright went again to the engine-room voice-pipe. The Chief Engineer answered. 'Captain here, Chief. Enemy in sight. I shall take avoiding action.' He slammed down the voice-pipe cover. He turned to the Chief Officer, who had reported to the bridge. 'Mr Hennessey, swing out all boats, passengers to muster at their boat stations.'

Tom was watching the emerging warship closely. He reported, 'She's signalling, sir.' There was a series of flashes from the German's flag deck, the international call sign. Then more flashes, Tom read them off. 'She's ordering us to heave to, sir.'

'Is she, by God! Well, she can read my answer for herself. I take no orders from the enemy. Wheel hard a-port, Mr Chatto, and ring down for emergency full ahead on the engines.'

Under full helm, the *Orsino* began to swing. That was when the shelling started. Speed was now of the essence;

Fullbright needed more power below, more and more coal shovelled faster and faster into the furnace mouths. Even with the off-watch firemen roused out to go below, there would not be enough hands.

'I'll call for volunteers,' Fullbright said. The word was passed below. The response, under threat of the German guns, was good. The Frenchmen, other passengers and stewards stripped to the waist and went down to the bowels of the ship. By superhuman effort from all hands, the speed was quickly increased until, unbelievably, it reached eighteen knots.

The German gunnery was good: that was one aspect in which the German Navy was superior to the British. Plumes of water rose along the port and starboard sides of the liner. The German, now positively identified as the *Dresden*, closed the distance. But Fullbright had in fact had a start on her, the lookout having reported again, this time to the effect that the German had been coaling ship from a collier, and had had to detach before getting under way. Fullbright hastily scanned the chart with Tom Chatto. The first business of a shipmaster with passengers aboard, with no guns or armour to protect them, was to make himself scarce. There was no dishonour in that. And the Marshals of France would be wanting their military reservists intact. Even the liner's current eighteen knots would be overtaken by the *Dresden*'s twenty-one-plus if the German didn't sink her first. There was only one thing for it.

'We're close to the strait, Chatto. We'll go in and hide –'

'But she can follow us in. A rat in a trap –'

'I don't like the analogy, but you're right.' Fullbright pondered on the chart, knowing that he had little time left. God's grace alone was keeping the shells from striking. 'So many uncharted waters behind Cape Horn . . .'

'Which makes that our best chance, sir.'

Fullbright looked up. 'Meaning?'

'The uncharted waters, sir. Where the *Dresden* isn't likely to risk entry.' Tom laid a pencil-tip on the chart. 'Cape St George, sir. A good shielding promontory, outside the Magellan Strait itself. There's a possibility of waterways leading off, those uncharted waterways might lead through to Punta Arenas.' Tom looked up. 'Worth a chance, sir?'

'Risky. Very risky.' Fullbright had heard reports originating from the few inhabitants of that terrible region. A nightmare for navigators to be sure . . . a place filled with rocky pinnacles and reefs, with dangerous currents swirling around, with overfalls and tide-rips abounding. Worth a risk? Maybe it offered a chance, a better chance than the German guns. Fullbright looked up again as a spout of water rose on the port bow and sent spray flinging over the fore well-deck and the bridge itself. Closer and closer . . . and the boom and roar of the guns also concentrated the mind wonderfully. The falls of shot had been close enough to send shock waves through the ship, making her plates ring. Below, the Chief Officer and the carpenter would be sounding round for sprung plates leading to leaks and other damage, but no reports had come to the bridge. All well – but for how much longer?

Fullbright reached his decision. 'Very well, Chatto. Cape St George it is. Then we shall see.'

Going back to the bridge from the charthouse, he passed the orders to head the ship in behind the high promontory of Cape St George. The shelling continued but refuge was not far off. As the liner passed at eighteen knots behind the massive rock, the gunfire stopped. It could be little more than a temporary respite, but a respite it was. The German was not following in behind them. Not yet. Fullbright wondered what the German Captain's thoughts might be; he could suspect a trap and was showing caution. He wouldn't know for sure the disposition of the British South Atlantic squadron, the *Good Hope* and the *Monmouth*, both armoured cruisers carrying 6-inch turreted guns as their main armament. Meanwhile it would be Fullbright's job to reassure his passengers and crew and to make decisions ahead, whether or not to risk his 9000-ton command in those uncharted waters as suggested by his navigator, Tom Chatto.

He brought his ship up in the sheltered lee of the cape, and she lay there as Fullbright manoeuvred his engines at dead slow ahead and astern to maintain position a mere cable's length from the bottom of the rock. For obvious reasons, he would not use his anchors. But the German, it seemed after a while, was not prepared to risk entry.

TWO

THE RESERVISTS, BEING FRENCH, WERE excitable. There was much talk, not to say panic, among them and the civilian passengers. The most senior of the reserve soldiers, a colonel not yet back in uniform, sought out the Captain, appearing on the bridge without prior permission shortly after the ship had eased engines. In the circumstances Fullbright refrained from despatching him summarily back down the ladder.

'*Capitaine*, my troops wish to get back to France quickly. Also they are anxious for their safety against the German –'

'I can offer no panaceas, Colonel, and as to a quick arrival in France, well, we're facing *force majeure*. We may have to wait upon the German's convenience. I have no choice currently. But be assured we'll not remain here for ever.' Fullbright, a large man with the authority of the four gold stripes on the shoulders of his bridge coat, and his gold-oak-leafed cap, standing on his own bridge where he was, in official Board of Trade terms, Master under God, loomed over the colonel, who was a small skinny man with a loud voice and an irritatingly bombastic manner. 'I shall keep you informed, never fear –'

'But do you not, for Heaven's sake, realize –'

'There are no buts,' Fullbright said crisply, 'and I realize many things. The situation is under control for now.' And what of the future? he thought to himself. However, he wasn't going to speak of the future just yet. 'Inform your troops, if you please, Colonel, that I fully understand their yen for home, which is where I aim to take them safely in due course. Now if you'll kindly leave my bridge I have many matters of urgency to attend to.'

'But *Capitaine*, I must protest strongly –'

Fullbright lifted an arm and pointed towards the starboard ladder. With an ill grace the Frenchman took the hint and, muttering away to himself, went below. Fullbright turned to the Chief Officer. 'I must speak to the passengers and crew, Mr Hennessey, without too much delay. They'll need calming after that experience. Pass the word, if you please, for all passengers, and heads of departments not immediately required for duty, to muster in the first-class lounge in half an hour's time.'

Hennessey saluted and turned away. 'One moment, Mr Hennessey. When you've passed my orders on, I'll want you to be on the bridge during my absence below. I'm to be informed at once if there's any movement, any sign of the *Dresden*.'

All the passengers were assembled; and the muster was attended by the First Officer and junior deck officers, the purser, the doctor, the Second Engineer in place of the Chief Engineer standing by on the starting-platform below; also the chief and second stewards together with the bosun, the carpenter and the two masters-at-arms in charge of the ship's police and general crew discipline.

Fullbright gave them the simple facts as known. 'It is likely the *Dresden* will remain on station outside the cape, waiting for us to come out, which we shall not do. On the other hand, her Captain will be aware in a general sense that there is a British naval squadron in the South Atlantic, under the command of Rear-Admiral Sir Christopher Cradock, so discretion may be seen as the better part of valour, to coin a phrase.' Fullbright smiled, his manner easy and relaxed. 'Now, I realize that the very name of the *Dresden* is somewhat charged . . . she has had a good deal of success as a commerce raider and there's no point in my glossing over that. But I do not believe that any of our lives are at risk. The officers of the German Navy are, after all, known to behave as gentlemen and to observe, *mostly* at any rate – I have the U-boats in mind – the customs, traditions and chivalry of the sea. Never mind the recent shelling which took place out at sea in open water, and was intended only to force me to heave to. They will not, I truly believe, attack a merchant ship seeking refuge in Chilean waters –'

'We could be approached by them and taken prisoner, *Capitaine*, could we not?' The interruption came from the French colonel. Fullbright agreed that this could happen if the German was prepared to breach the conventions of Chilean neutrality to that extent, but said that this was a matter for the future and he would be considering what might be done to circumvent such a possibility.

'A stratagem, *Capitaine*?'

'A stratagem, Colonel, yes.'

The word seemed to please the Frenchman. Leaving the lounge after dealing with a number of questions, largely querulous ones, and stressing that the passengers must at all times obey the orders of the ship's company, Fullbright went back to the bridge. He called to Tom.

'Mr Chatto, a moment.'

'Sir?'

'I am called upon to produce a stratagem . . . like a rabbit from a hat! I have some thoughts, but first it seems to me that we need to know the actual current whereabouts of the *Dresden* – that's to say, whether or not she's still outside. She may have done a bunk ahead of Cradock's squadron. I'd like you to take the seaboat away at first light tomorrow and carry out a reconnaissance. Keeping yourself as far out of sight as possible, I need scarcely say . . .'

As the dawn came up the seaboat was lowered on the falls and slipped on to icy cold water, lying calm and flat beneath the loom of the mountainous terrain. Tom took only the seaboat's crew with him. Under muffled oars the boat was pulled away from the ship's side as silently as possible: sounds carry well across water. It was an eerie feeling, to lie on a fjord-like inlet at the feet of the massive mountains with the German cruiser doubtless still not far off. All the reservists and other passengers lined the open decks: they maintained strict silence, a difficult task for the French who had been explicitly warned by the purser and stewards, backed by orders from the Chief Officer.

Coming up to the point of land below the overhang of the cliff, a spit that would provide a makeshift jetty for the seaboat and a vantage point from which Tom hoped to get a view of the open water beyond, he jumped ashore and made his way to the far side of the spit, keeping concealed by scrub and boulders. He inched up from cover, slowly, carefully, though he was unlikely to be seen in the early light with the sun scarcely yet visible.

There was the *Dresden*, a dark shape steaming slowly up and down. Waiting, ready to close the trap as soon as the *Orsino* put her nose outside Cape St George. There was no way out in that direction. Tom went back across the spit of land and the seaboat's crew pulled back to the liner to be hooked on to the falls and hoisted.

'Well, now we know,' Fullbright said when Tom reported. 'It has to be the uncharted waters.' There were a number of channels leading off the wide water behind the cape. 'We'll not know where we're going from one moment to the next and we'll not know where we'll end up. But we stake everything on the chance of finding the strait – by the back door, so to speak, since the German stops us using the front. I'll go in behind a line of soundings, Mr Chatto, and that's where you come in. I propose sending you away in the seaboat with your yeoman. You'll take soundings continually, reporting them back to me each time. I'll follow behind you, with my engines at dead slow. That's the best we can do, and it's going to be by guess and by God since we haven't the remotest idea, as I've said, where we'll be going – or what we might hit beneath the surface. Apart from God, Mr Chatto, it's going to be entirely up to you. I trust you not to put my ship aground . . . I have every confidence that you'll not do that. Is all that understood?'

'Yes, sir.'

'Good! Then we'll lose no time. We shall call this the stratagem demanded by the Frenchman.' Fullbright passed orders down for the seaboat to stand by again. He spoke on the voice-pipe to the Chief Engineer on the starting-platform below, urging immediate response to all engine orders from the bridge. After making his preparations Tom went to the seaboat's falls and, with his yeoman carrying a leadline, was lowered to the water and slipped. The seaboat was pulled ahead by its crew as the liner turned towards what Fullbright and Tom had decided was as good a place to start as any: an inlet wide enough to take the liner's beam, though currently God alone knew whether or not the depth of water would be enough to take her draught. From now on, every move could prove a threat to the ship. Indeed it began to seem a crazy scheme, risky in the extreme, one almost bound to end in disaster when set against the normal standards and requirements of sane ship-handling. Tom knew well, as did Fullbright, that the liner's bottom plating could be ripped out on a shoal, on jagged, submerged rock that might have missed the cast of the leadline.

His heart virtually in his mouth as the seaboat nosed into the inlet and his yeoman cast the lead time after time, thus far showing enough water for the great bulk of the liner to nose in after them, Tom looked at his surroundings with awe. Soon they were lost, literally, in the maze of the waterways, moving on slowly beneath the mountains of the Andes chain, in the Fuegan archipelago, a thousand miles farther south than the latitude of the Cape of Good Hope, as Tom reminded himself, a thousand miles closer to the South Polar icefields . . . it was the most dismal region in the world, cold and forlorn, virtually uninhabited except for a handful of natives, semi-naked during their brief summers, a territory in which until now no ship had penetrated to attempt the myriad channels, a silent territory except when the great westerly gales blew around the vicinity of Cape Horn, a territory always menacing in its lost vastness.

There was little conversation in the seaboat as the mountains closed in around them. Just the monotony of the repeated soundings, time and again as the liner virtually inched on behind them: 'Deep eight . . . by the mark ten . . . and a quarter five . . . and a quarter less thirteen . . .' In the time-honoured vocabulary of soundings by hand leadline the fathoms were called out and reported back to Fullbright as the markings, curious to a landsman, were seen at the waterline each time the line came up and down: two tails of leather in the line signified two fathoms; a piece of white linen showed five fathoms; a piece of leather with a hole indicated ten fathoms, a piece of blue serge thirteen. Every now and again, as Tom's boat covered from port to starboard, or starboard to port, the lead would show a dangerous lack of water, and Tom would use his megaphone.

'Nothing to port . . . shoaling water!'

Fullbright handled his ship with minute precision, calmly. At any moment, for all anyone could tell, the ship might strike some submerged rock and she could go hard aground with water pouring in through torn plates.

It was touch-and-go; or more accurately in the circumstances it was touch-and-don't-go, Tom thought sardonically to himself. The line was heaved almost continuously when it found shoaling water, the reports going back to Fullbright sometimes by hand signals, sometimes by use of the megaphone and, at night, by torchlight flashes.

Tom and his crew of six seamen and two leadsmen had prepared for a long spell; there had been no knowing how long they would need to spend in the open boat. They had brought warm clothing, watchcoats and oilskins and balaclavas, and woollen scarves and mittens. They had brought emergency rations, and barricoes of fresh water in addition to the normal equipment of a lifeboat. Stops were made at intervals, stops when Tom brought the boat back alongside the liner and hooked on to the falls for an exchange of boat's crew. Tom and his yeoman took turns at heaving the lead and reporting back, one of them at a time being able to snatch a little sleep, sleep that soon became a sleep of exhaustion. And the monotony of the task seemed to go on and on for ever and a day, with the constantly repeated soundings becoming like the chorus of an often-repeated song. There seemed to be no progress; Tom felt himself becoming an automaton, his limbs stiffening from the cramped position on the thwart. Endless, endless . . . one more inlet to try, then another leading off, then another; and not infrequently a boss-shot.

At one stage they were eight miles, by Tom's reckoning, up a channel, a zigzag, twisting channel just wide enough for the liner to follow down when, coming round one of the twists deep below the sheer sides of a mountain range, they found a great white icy mass blocking the way ahead.

'It's a bloody glacier, sir,' Tom's yeoman said in weary disgust. Tom felt like weeping from sheer frustration and exhaustion. Soon after, as the *Orsino* came around the bend dead slow, Fullbright saw the blocking glacier for himself. He called down, using a megaphone, his words echoing off the blank rock-faces. 'Bad luck, Mr Chatto! Not your fault. There's no room to turn here. I'll come out astern. Move past me, and carry on leading.'

'A case of leading arse first,' the yeoman said gloomily. 'Or barse ackards, as they say.'

After that, another channel, another blocked exit or shoaling water, then another . . .

Five days, no less. Five days of hell and doubt; continual

doubt as to whether he had adequately covered the channel for the ship behind, whether some plate-ripping jag had gone undetected by the lead, resulting in that ripped bottom that had been on the cards all along, resulting in what would become a total loss at Lloyd's of London of a valuable 9000-ton Royal Mail ship.

Five days. Towards evening of the fifth day, the channel ahead lay straight and true, and in the distance Tom saw what he believed to be open water.

Open water it was, and just in time. The boat's crew were almost at the end of their endurance. The seaboat pulled on, with the liner behind, until Fullbright's megaphoned order came from the high bridge of the *Orsino*: 'Come alongside, Mr Chatto, hook on to the falls . . . you've done it! Punta Arenas is ahead. You have my congratulations . . . you and your crew . . . and my heartfelt thanks for not hazarding my ship!'

Back aboard, Tom slept, going out like a light when, after a man-sized tot of whisky, his head hit the pillow in his bunk. At Punta Arenas at the South Atlantic exit from the Magellan Strait, wireless contact was made by HMS *Glasgow*, proceeding south from Rio de Janeiro. An officer from the *Glasgow* boarded the liner in due course and was given the story. He brought word that the pursuit was on of the German East Asiatic Squadron of which the *Dresden* had been a detached unit. The outcome, not long after, was the battle of Coronel and the tragic loss of Sir Christopher Cradock, his flagship the *Good Hope*, and the armoured cruiser *Monmouth*.

This news, greeted in Britain almost with disbelief, reached the *Orsino* whilst on passage from Punta Arenas to the Mersey. It came as a grievous blow to all aboard, and Fullbright was much saddened. Cradock had been known as a fine seaman, respected in the merchant ships as much as in the King's ships.

'They'll be avenged,' he said. 'Never doubt that for a moment.'

THREE

News of the incident with the German ship and the almost impossible feat of seamanship had spread: the *Orsino* entered the Mersey to a civic welcome and a good deal of fuss. Fullbright, who had saved a great many lives, not least those of the French reservists who would live on to fight for the glory of their country, was honoured by both the British and French governments. Not long after the liner's arrival his prophecy was vindicated: on 8 December a British squadron under Admiral Sturdee met von Spee at the Falkland Islands, sinking the *Scharnhorst*, the *Gneisenau*, the *Leipzig* and the *Nürnberg*, the *Dresden* alone escaping the British guns.

Two weeks after the Liverpool arrival, Tom Chatto had taken his leave of the *Orsino*. He had been interviewed by the Board of PSNC and had confirmed to them his decision to apply for a commission in the Royal Naval Reserve; thence he had attended an Admiralty Board in London and had been granted a commission as temporary sub-lieutenant with a guarantee of promotion to lieutenant on completion of naval training. He spent a week in a London hotel while his uniforms were converted to the naval pattern and he awaited his first appointment. When this reached him he went by train from Waterloo to Portsmouth with orders to report to HMS *Excellent*, the naval gunnery school at Whale Island where he would learn the rudiments of sea weaponry.

Whale Island, he found, was a place of movement at the double, of gaitered gunners' mates who screeched orders apparently without cease, of marching and counter-marching, of rifle drill and sword drill and the handling of naval artillery of all calibres. The long gunnery course, normally lasting two years, had been suspended at the outbreak of war; the regular RN sub-lieutenants underwent a shortened course, while those of the RNR and the Royal Naval Volunteer Reserve were grouped together in an intensive three-week course designed to give no more than a smattering of knowledge sufficient for them to understand the broad principles of gunnery.

No matter whether you were RN, RNR or RNVR, all were Officers Under Training; as such, their God had to be the parade chief gunner's mate, a chief petty officer who strode about loudly, his back ramrod-straight, his eye taking in the smallest detail of correct dress, of cack-handedness, of inattention on parade. To Tom, it all smacked more of the army than of the navy; he was a seaman and a navigator, not a gunner or a tailor's dummy in a brassbound uniform. After a few days, he began to regret the intertwined gold lace of the RNR on his cuff.

There was, however, a recompense: one of his brother officers, Peter Mason, who had overlapped into Tom's course from an earlier one, was an acquaintance from the past. Mason like himself had come from the PSNC, though the two had never served together. Together now, they could commiserate.

'Too much bullshit,' Mason said bitterly after a morning's parade-ground drill. 'Gunners' mates . . . all gate and gaiters. Not born of woman. They were quarried.' He paused. 'You were Second on the *Orsino* when she made that crazy passage – right? It was you who took the soundings.'

Tom nodded.

'That was brilliant. Old Fullbright got a lot of kudos from that. British and French honours. I don't remember hearing anything coming in your direction, Chatto.'

Tom shrugged. 'No reason why it should. Fullbright was

the one who took the risk. If I'd made a balls of it . . . it would have been his ship lost, and his the blame.'

'Well – perhaps. But still. Anyway – have you got leave tonight?'

Tom had; so had Peter Mason. 'Then let's go ashore, get out of this hell-hole. The Queen's Hotel in Southsea is the place to go. Wine, women and song. All very respectable, of course, but you never know your luck.'

Portsmouth was a place of very many public houses for the ratings from the RN barracks in Queen Street and from the ships in the dockyard. Tom and Peter Mason took the tram from Whale Island to Edinburgh Road, disembarking outside the Royal Sailors' Rest, known as Aggie Weston's after its founder. This was a place where naval ratings, far from home, could get a bed for a tanner a night with meals to match the price, and no questions asked. Miss Weston was a teetotaller and a strict one, but her Royal Sailors' Rests never turned away a drunken sailor, possibly in the knowledge that if they did they would never get a customer . . . Tom and Mason made their way along Edinburgh Road, past the Neptune Gate into the dockyard, then along Queen Street. They came past the huge sprawl of the naval barracks with its wide parade-ground flanked by the tall seamen's blocks and an armed guard on the gate beside the guardroom presided over by the gunner's mate of the watch and the duty master-at-arms or regulating petty officer. As they came past the gate a stream of ratings emerged, wearing their best Number One uniforms with gold badges and lanyards.

'Libertymen,' Mason remarked. 'Bound for the nearest pub. Or knocking-shop.' He laughed. 'All ashore that's going ashore – remember? And remember that in the RN you don't leave barracks – you go ashore.'

Tom had been told that already, at lectures by the Executive Officer of *Excellent* and the Commander (G) as a preliminary to the course. That, and other things peculiar to the RN. In barracks, as aboard a ship in the dockyard, ratings caught 'libertyboats' rather than just walked through the gate; each 'libertyboat' left at a regular time and if a man missed it he had to wait for the next one. As the men fell in to catch the libertyboat they were inspected to ensure the correct wearing of uniform, and were inspected again on their return to barracks for signs of drunkenness, though since the outbreak of war many a blind eye had been turned to insobriety unless the man was fighting drunk. The RN maintained an iron-hard discipline in general, but there was humanity and understanding as well.

Tom and Peter Mason walked on, keeping step as drilled into them by the hierarchy of the gunnery school: officers must at all times set an example. Salutes were returned to right and left as naval ratings and soldiers passed them. This, Tom was to find, was just one of the irksome parts of the compulsory wartime wearing of uniform. And the setting of examples was not always easy: halfway along Queen Street, where every other establishment seemed to be either a naval outfitter's or a public house filled to the doors with bluejackets, a large crowd of girls, mostly in their early twenties and wearing overalls, surged out from a doorway to what looked like a clothing workroom. The girls were in high spirits, laughing, pushing each other, singing. They swept down on the two officers, linking arms with them, all of them together now bursting into the current music-hall song.

'All the nice girls love a sailor,
All the nice girls love a tar,
All the nice girls love a sailor,
For you know what sailors are . . .'

They were borne along on an exuberant wave of friendliness. Tom's face was taken in a pair of hands and he was given a smacking kiss. They were besieged, virtually helpless until a loud voice roared out from the other side of the road where a naval patrol, four seamen with side-arms and gaiters under a petty officer, marched in the gutter, on the lookout for trouble.

'Cut it out, ladies! Behave yourselves. Stop molesting the officers, all right?'

There were hoots and catcalls, loud comments about interfering bastards who were too old to enjoy themselves; but the girls released Tom and Peter Mason and moved on towards Edinburgh Road.

The petty officer marched up, arms swinging, and halted in front of the two reservists. He saluted. 'No offence, gentlemen, but you want to watch your step in certain parts of Pompey Town. If you'll take my advice, gentlemen, you'll not walk along Queen Street once night leave's been piped in the barracks. A tram from Commercial Road into Southsea would be just the ticket.'

Tom felt rebuked. He said, 'I'm sure you're right, PO. And – thank you.'

The petty officer saluted again. 'No bother, sir.' He turned about and marched back to his waiting patrol. Mason said, 'We'd better do as daddy says.' The petty officer was a man in his fifties, obviously a recalled RFR man, a fleet reservist. 'He's right, of course. What he might have said but didn't was that officers shouldn't risk a shindig with drunken matloes. Makes sense – but we won't turn about now. It's not far to the main gate of the dockyard.'

Reaching the Hard outside the main gate, they turned past Gieves, the naval officers' tailors, and the Keppel's Head Hotel, then Mason led the way across the tram tracks towards the harbour station. Across the road they looked down on a large area of deep, liquid black mud extending from the wall of the Hard up to the supports of the railway line to Waterloo.

'Mudlarks,' Mason said. 'Just watch.'

A number of filthy urchins of ages apparently ranging from five to fifteen stood waist-deep in the mud, some twenty feet below, calling up to the passers-by. Mason reached into a pocket and brought out a penny. This he threw down into the mud. The urchins ploughed about in search of it, almost vanishing from sight as they did so. In the poor light thrown by the railway station's lamps and the lamp standards on the Hard, the penny must surely have been invisible; but there was a shout of triumph as one of the muddy figures came up with it. Tom felt in his pocket and came up with a half-crown. He hesitated for a moment since a half-crown was a lot out of a sub-lieutenant's pay, then threw it. A bigger boy caught it in flight.

'Thanks, mister, you're a toff!'

Tom smiled and lifted a hand in acknowledgement. As he did so an elderly woman with a large, flowery hat held down by a lace veil secured beneath her chin crossed the road from the Keppel's Head and, alongside Tom, stared down towards the mud. 'You should *not* encourage them,' she reproved in a severe tone. 'They're an *absolute disgrace.*' She leaned over the rail. 'You are a lot of horrid, dirty little boys,' she said loudly. 'I think the police should deal with you – and your parents for allowing you out.'

This was not well received. 'Silly old bitch,' came up equally loudly. 'Stinkin' old cow.' Then another voice: 'Garn, yer fuckin' old busybody, we're bloody *traditional*, so *sucks*!'

The woman glared speechlessly, then, finding her tongue, she rounded on Tom and Mason. 'Such impertinence, such *language*. And how on earth is it that such common children even know the word traditional?'

The question was rhetorical. The woman flounced away. Tom watched her sardonically. He was thinking of the urchins in that appalling mud, thinking of how much one single penny must mean to them. He had seen poverty in the South American ports – Rio de Janeiro, Montevideo, Buenos Aires, Valparaiso – and had seen it in Liverpool too in the areas by the docks. But he had never had it brought home to him quite so vividly as now. Two halves, the haves and the have-nots, here in the heart of the Empire, the home of the British Navy. It was likely enough that those urchins' fathers were seamen in the fleet, risking their lives in dangerous waters – for their sons to exist like this. Tom wondered, in a moment of self-guilt, why it was that some people found the country worth fighting for.

Mason gave him a nudge. 'Come back to Pompey, old boy! We now move on to where the toffs hang out.'

They caught another tram and were deposited close to the vast building of the Queen's Hotel, all elegance and comfort behind the sergeant-majorly presence of the frock-coated head porter.

The bar was filled with naval officers, mostly the younger ones and mostly accompanied by young ladies. The older and more senior officers – the hotel seemed to be all navy – sat with their more mature ladies, who might or might not have been their wives. Tom recalled what he had been told was the time-honoured toast in the wardrooms of the fleet when at sea on Saturday nights: 'To our sweethearts and wives. May they never meet.'

'Gin,' Mason said as they approached the bar. 'That's the one common factor, I'm told, between the seniors and juniors, the wardroom and the gunroom. Gin and plenty of it. A penny a tot duty-free at sea – well, we know that, of course.'

He paid for two double gins: a good deal more than twopence each in the Queen's Hotel; among other considerations, you paid for the comfort. They retired to a corner. Tom saw that Mason had a roving eye and was using it frequently, though none of the young ladies was unattached. Mason remarked on this. 'I did speak of wine, women and song, did I not?'

'You did.'

'But I did add that the Queen's is a respectable place. So you're out of luck on that score, old boy. That's if you're interested.' He produced a silver cigarette-case and offered it to Tom. They lit up; Peter Mason blew a stream of smoke. 'And I rather believe you are.'

'What d'you mean?'

Mason smiled blandly. 'Gossip, old boy. The good old PSNC . . . a hotbed of gossip one way and another.'

Tom's voice was cold. 'Do go on.'

'Well . . . it's just that PSNC's a small world. When I was in the *Osorno* a while ago, a little bird sang a song. If you follow? No?'

'I think you'd better tell me more.'

'Righto, then.' Mason paused, took a mouthful of gin. 'We had a homeward passenger, a Mrs Handley. Grace Handley. Embarked at Valparaiso.'

'So?'

'She knew you, Chatto. In the *Orvega*. Yes?'

'Yes, that's right enough. She was – a pleasant enough woman.'

'Yes, she was. She had plenty of time for you, you know.'

Tom didn't comment.

Mason went on, 'But you were already fixed up – she said. I gather there was an Argentinian lass.'

Tom blew out his cheeks. So that was the way the conversation was leading. It was some relief. 'Correct,' he said. 'Dolores Pontarena. Her father was a rancher out there. Beef.'

'Plenty of money.'

'Yes.'

Mason was silent for a moment; then he asked, 'But do I take it, it didn't work out?'

'No, it didn't.'

Mason shook his head. 'All that money.'

'All that beef.'

'H'm? Oh – I get it, old boy. Prospective father-in-law wanted to take you over?'

'He wanted me to leave the sea. So did Dolores. The sea's

my life. I never had any intention of leaving it, certainly not for life in a beefscreen.'

Mason burst out laughing. 'Not exactly a beefscreen,' he said, the reference being to the frozen beef storage aboard a ship. 'One day, you'd have copped a golden store.'

'Probably. Old Pontarena had no sons.'

'Then you're a bloody fool if you don't mind my saying so, old boy –'

'I said I wasn't interested. I told you, I wouldn't leave the sea.'

Mason shook his head in wonderment. 'Well, I suppose it takes all sorts. The PSNC'd not have seen my arse for dust if I'd had your chance.' He added, 'Of course, it would depend on the girl . . .'

'Well, anyway, let's drop it, shall we? Another gin?'

'Thanks, old boy.' Mason held out his glass; Tom went to the bar. When he returned with the two gins Mason was staring through the doorway into the reception lobby. He looked thunderstruck and at the same time intrigued.

'Talk of the devil,' he said.

'What?'

'What we were on about, old boy.'

'Pontarena?'

'Not Pontarena. Grace Handley.'

Grace Handley had come into the bar. She was alone; Tom found all sorts of emotions running through him. Though in her late thirties now, she was still attractive, still didn't look her age. The years in Chile had not dried her up.

She saw Tom almost instantly, as though drawn towards him, he thought. She recognized Peter Mason as well; she came across, hands outstretched in greeting. 'Well,' she said. 'Not just one ghost from the past, but two.' She looked at their RNR stripes. 'The link,' she said. 'That's why you're both here. Not such a coincidence after all. Tell me, how are you both after so long? The *Orvega* and the *Osorno*, wasn't it?

As though I could forget.' She was looking particularly at Tom; and he noticed the quizzical look Peter Mason gave him.

FOUR

QUITE SOON, PETER MASON SAW THAT he was superfluous. He excused himself and Tom watched him heading out of the bar towards a girl in the uniform of a naval nursing sister, a member of Queen Alexandra's Royal Naval Nursing Service, standing at reception. Tom grinned when he saw an obvious father or uncle appear at her side.

Grace Handley put a hand on Tom's arm. She had been observing him closely. It was some four years since they had last been in contact. In that time, Tom had matured a lot. There was plenty of assurance in his manner – no flamboyance like his friend Peter Mason, but a quiet confidence and an air of command about him now that spoke of a readiness to take charge in any emergency. With the added years, he had if anything gained attraction for her. She asked, 'How have things been, love?'

'Pretty good,' he said. He told her his last PSNC ship had been the *Orsino*. She had read in the newspapers about that encounter with the *Dresden*, and the nightmare at the world's bottom that had followed. They talked of that for a while, then she asked about Dolores, and he told her about that too.

'A lucky escape,' she said. 'I saw her and her father that day they came aboard at Puerto Montt, when we put in for repairs, remember?'

'Yes. Engine-room breakdown.' He grinned. 'D'you remember Lady Moyra Bentinck?'

'*Wasn't* she frightful, Tom? That poor little Irish maid of hers . . . But tell me more about yourself, Tom. Have you been back home to Ireland?'

'Yes, I have – since I saw you last. Not very recently. But I'll get leave waiting appointment when I've finished at Whale Island.' He told her of the gunnery and naval initiation course for officers of the reserves. 'Gunnery's about the lot for us, for the RNR people. We're assumed to know enough about navigation and ship-handling, general seamanship . . . after all, most of us have our masters' certificates.'

She nodded, moved a little closer. 'Do you like it, Tom? The navy?'

He reflected. 'They're a stuffy bunch, a lot of them, the RN straight-stripers. But it's not too bad.' He paused, scanning her face. She had definitely not aged. 'Tell me about yourself, Grace.'

'Well,' she said, looking down at her lap. 'You'll remember I spoke of my husband. I expect I told you he was . . . rather old for me.'

'Yes.' He remembered she had referred to him as a dry old stick.

She gave a small chuckle. 'He's older now. And yes, since you ask, we're still married. I think I said at the time, civil servants don't get divorced. Anyway, I was going out to join my sister in Chile. She had connections; I thought she could get me a job. Well, she couldn't as it turned out. And I found that it doesn't pay to live with a sister. So I came back. And rejoined my husband.'

'He's still in the civil service?'

'Yes, he is, Tom. The war extended his service. But he's had a shift of department. He's to do with supplies.' She gave him a quick glance from lowered lashes. 'Naval supplies. He was sent here to Portsmouth. Hence me, you see.'

Tom, feeling vaguely uncomfortable, murmured something about coincidence.

'Yes, isn't it,' she said. 'He works in the dockyard. Usually.' She paused, then took a deep breath. 'As it happens, he's up north for a while, six weeks, in Rosyth. Setting up an organization, he calls it.'

Tom nodded. Most of the main fleets had left the southern ports, Portsmouth, Chatham and Devonport, on the outbreak of the war. The great battleships and battle-cruisers, when not at sea, spent their time swinging round the buoys in the Clyde, or the Firth of Forth off Rosyth, or in the Moray Firth and Scapa Flow in the Orkneys, the latter a barren, windswept area only sparsely populated.

They were silent for a moment or two; then Grace said with a touch of unaccustomed shyness, 'We have a flat. Just now, *I* have a flat. It's quite near here. Just round the corner in fact, Shaftesbury Road. There's a maid, but she's a daily. I'm alone at night.'

Tom cleared his throat. She looked at him quizzically, saw his embarrassment. She said rather crossly, 'Oh God, Tom, you're a big boy now. But you haven't changed, have you? I'm sorry if I've been too forward.'

He flushed. 'No – no, you haven't, Grace.' She looked so pathetic, he thought, so defenceless if that was the word. 'It's just that – that – oh, I don't know really. Call me a fool if you like, but . . .'

'*I* know,' she said, 'if you don't. Other men's wives?'

Feeling he'd let her down, he said miserably, 'Perhaps, yes.'

She patted his knee again. 'That's what comes of having a parson for a father. Parsons' sons either go wild when they leave home – booze and floozies, not that I'm a floozie, Tom, or they remain stuck with the vicarage. You're in the latter category, aren't you? But there wouldn't be any harm in my cooking you dinner, or anyway supper. Would there?'

He smiled. 'No harm at all,' he said.

Tom went back to Whale Island that night, in time to catch the last tram that would get him back aboard by midnight. He had enjoyed Grace's simple cooking; she had made the best use of the food available: some shortages were already becoming noticeable and it was likely there would one day be rationing. Nothing that Tom's father the Dean would have called 'untoward' had taken place. Tom as a normal man had felt the urges; but Grace had not tried again to force anything. And Tom had controlled his instincts. It had not been just the thought of a husband absent from home on service for his country, though that had weighed. It had been more the sheer practicalities of the situation. A time might well come when sex would lose its dangers; there had been publicity – adverse publicity it had to be admitted – given to a certain Mrs Marie Stopes, who appeared to have the answers. But her time had not yet come, and Tom was unwilling to risk Grace becoming pregnant when he had no intention afterwards of doing the decent thing, becoming co-respondent in a divorce case and then marrying her, having in the meantime wrecked a man's civil service career and possibly jeopardized his RNR commission as well.

But as he travelled back in the tram's clangour to the gunnery school, his mind was in a turmoil. He slept little that night. Before first parade next morning Peter Mason laid a hand on his shoulder.

'Well, old man? How did you make out last night, h'm?' His look was lecherous. Tom snapped at him to mind his own bloody business. But, in deference to Grace Handley, he added, 'I didn't *make out* as you term it.'

'Bad luck, old man!'

'Oh, push off, for God's sake.'

He was slow on parade that day, fluffing an about-turn. The course was halted, turned into line, and Tom was approached by the petty officer gunner's mate, gaitered and belted and with his cap on very straight. 'Well now, Mr Chatto, sir, we're a little on the *lazy* side this morning, aren't we? We seem to have had a bad night. Tell me, sir: were you ashore last night?'

'Yes, PO.'

'Ha! Perhaps that explains our lack of co-ordination this morning, Mr Chatto. In future we must ensure that our *activities* away from the ship do not lead to any lack of *concentration*, must we not, sir?'

'Yes, PO.'

'Good! Now then, gentlemen, allow me to give you all some advice, such as a father might give.' The gunner's mate took a deep breath and a pace to the rear. '*Tie a knot in it, it saves heartache.* Right? Now, gentlemen, if you'll kindly pay attention to your hard-done-by but nevertheless well-meaning instructor . . . into file, *right* turn, form *fours* . . . double *march* . . .'

The gruelling day proceeded, ending at 1600 hours with the supervised stripping-down of a 6-inch gun.

They met again. More than once. Grace Handley was the only person Tom knew in the Portsmouth area. When, after a fortnight, a day's leave was given to the officers under training they went in a green tram of the Horndean Light Railway out to Cosham, little more than a village to the north of Portsea Island. They walked past a chalkpit to the top of Portsdown Hill, past the great forts – Southwick, Nelson, Widley with their vast guns manned by men of the Royal Garrison Artillery and facing seaward over the dockyard – built in the last century by order of Lord Palmerston against any threat from France. It was a fine, crisp day with high cloud and little wind. Grace had packed sandwiches and had brought a vacuum flask of coffee. They sat in a hollow beneath the crest of the hill, looking out over the dockyard with a number of light cruisers and torpedo-boat destroyers lying in the basins or at buoys in the stream. There was a solitary battle-cruiser alongside the wall at the South Railway jetty, HMS *Invincible* that had been Admiral Sturdee's flagship at the Falkland Islands battle. Soon, Tom would be away at sea again, perhaps aboard one of those ships.

Grace asked what appointment he expected to get.

'I've really no idea. We're entirely at the disposal of the Admiralty. All I can say is, I'm likely to get a navigator's berth rather than, say, gunnery. Or torpedoes. Or signals. Navigation's what I'm trained for.'

She nodded. She seemed sad; she would miss him badly, she said, and there was not long to go now. The picnic eaten, they walked towards Fareham and Porchester, descending the hill. In Fareham there was a diversion: four able seamen, already drunk, their arms linked, roaring out a song:

'Be Oi Pompey?
Be Oi buggery!
Oi belong to Fareham.
That's where the girls wear calico drawers
An' Oi be the bugger to tear 'em . . .'

Grace said with a giggle, 'Some girls are lucky.'

Two days later a letter came to Whale Island for Tom. A brief note to say Grace's husband was coming south sooner than expected. He was due back that night. Tom understood that that was that; but the note ended with the hope that it was only *au revoir*, that they would meet again before the war was over; and there were three crosses and a suspicious-looking splodge.

The following week saw the end of the gunnery course. There was a series of interviews with various RN officers and they were all quizzed as to how they saw their immediate future in naval service. Some wanted this, others that. Tom had no particular preference; only a desire to be done with training and get to sea as quickly as possible. It was stressed that what they wanted was not necessarily what they would get. The Admiralty was, as Tom had said to Grace, the arbiter. It was hoped that not too many square pegs would find themselves in round holes, but such was the way of the navy. So far as the lower deck was concerned, at any rate, Tom had heard weird tales: professional cooks, joining as Hostilities Only ratings, had been drafted as stokers; men who had worked as seamen locally on the Isle of Wight ferries found themselves turned into officers' stewards. And so on and so forth. Tom could only hope for the best, hope he wouldn't end up a dogsbody in a stone frigate, as the barracks and other shore establishments were known.

He needn't have worried: officers with master mariners' certificates were not all that thick on the ground now that the country had an ever-growing need to man more and more ships. Before finally leaving Whale Island on being given an abbreviated first-class certificate in gunnery, Tom was ordered to attend an interview in the wardroom block of the naval barracks.

He was admitted to a somewhat dingy room with the look of having been only recently fitted out as an office. There was little furniture beyond two desks, one large, the other small, and two upright chairs for the use of visitors. That, and a safe set securely into a wall.

At the smaller desk sat an assistant paymaster, an officer of the accountant branch of the navy. Behind the larger sat a captain RN, four straight stripes on his jacket cuffs and a brass hat hung on a hook behind him. The assistant paymaster got to his feet and introduced Tom.

'Lieutenant Chatto, sir.' Tom had already taken his uniforms – monkey-jackets, bridge coat, shoulder-straps for use with white uniforms for overseas stations – to Gieves on the Hard for the shipping of his second stripe.

'Ah, Chatto. Good morning – and welcome.' The Captain, who did not reveal his name, waved to a chair in front of his desk. 'Bring your arse to an anchor.'

'Thank you, sir.' Tom sat, and waited. The Captain seemed to be in no hurry. He brought out a pipe, filled it, and used a number of safety matches from a large box to light it. Then, puffing, he leaned back comfortably. He said, 'I've heard about that exploit behind Cape Horn. Remarkable, quite remarkable. I'd like to hear about it in your own words, Chatto.'

Tom told him. He nodded throughout, very blue eyes gazing into Tom's. When Tom had finished, the Captain said, 'Highly unorthodox. And very risky. How do you feel about it in retrospect?'

The question, sharply put, caught Tom off guard. He thought for a moment, then said simply, 'I feel very lucky, sir.'

The Captain smiled. 'I'm sure you do! Would you do something like that again?'

'I think I would, sir. In fact . . . well, it wasn't me who took the risk. My Captain took that . . . risking losing his ship.'

'You took a physical and professional risk and you came through, Chatto. It says much for your ability as a pilot.' He paused, puffing at his pipe and continuing to stare thoughtfully at Tom. Then he said abruptly, 'Now I'll come to the point. Your conduct in uncharted waters, your willingness to take a risk and to accept unorthodoxy has some bearing on what I'm going to say. On what I'm offering you. And I shall start by saying that all you hear in this room is classified Hush Most Secret. You understand that?'

The navy had various classifications of secrecy; in ascending order of importance these were Confidential, Secret, Most Secret and Hush Most Secret. The last classification was seldom used other than for such things as fleet movements or overall planning. When it was used in other contexts, the matter was to be treated as of the utmost importance.

'I understand, sir,' Tom said.

'Right. Now.' The Captain leaned forward, laying down his pipe. 'You'll no doubt be aware that the enemy submarines are causing serious losses to the fleet and are playing havoc with our merchant shipping in home waters and in the Mediterranean. Supply vessels coming in across the Atlantic, or homeward bound through the Suez Canal from Australia and New Zealand, are being picked off at a rate we simply cannot sustain for long. The country is totally dependent upon its imports, its basic supplies of food and oil amongst many other things. Of course, if you read the newspapers you'll be aware of all this. But I have to tell you – and I repeat in secrecy – that the newspapers do not tell half the story, because they're not allowed to by the censorship. It's vital, as you'll appreciate, not to alarm the civilian population.'

'Yes, sir.'

'But I can tell you this: if our merchant-ship losses continue at the present rate, the country will be starved out within a matter of months, maybe less. That, of course, is what the Hun is aiming at. The Kaiser's shipyards are turning out more and more U-boats . . . and our shipyards cannot produce sufficient quantities of torpedo-boat destroyers to cope with them, or to replace those lost, of which there have been many. So we have had to cast around for something else. We believe we have come up with the answer. I don't suppose you've heard of Commander Gordon Campbell?'

Tom shook his head. 'No, sir.'

'You will, in time. He's destined for flag rank, and one day may run the whole show. All this is his idea, his baby. And I'm appointing you to that baby of his, Chatto, for disposal.' The Captain gave a sudden laugh at the look on Tom's face. 'Don't be alarmed by the word disposal. You're not going to be flushed down the heads. It's just the navy's way of issuing an appointment without naming a precise ship – more or less that, anyway. Now – the "something else" we've come up with is what I might call mystery ships. Q ships, officially. Merchant vessels with concealed guns to act as lures to the enemy. Briefly, the task of the Q ship is to lie stopped when ordered to do so by a surfacing U-boat – if she hasn't been blown up by a torpedo first. That's the big risk, of course. But the ideal Q ship is one as nondescript as possible, such that a U-boat commander wouldn't waste a torpedo on her. He would come to the surface and attack by gunfire – shells are a lot cheaper than torpedoes, and a submarine can carry only a certain number of torpedoes in any case. So when the U-boat surfaces, the Q ship opens her gunport doors, runs up her battle ensigns – and opens fire. Preferably before the U-boat does the same. Caught with her trousers down, she's at an immediate disadvantage. That, at any rate is the hope.'

Tom was left with plenty to think about as he returned to Whale Island to await further orders. Q ships sounded rather too much like sitting ducks for his comfort, basically just hanging about waiting to be blown sky-high should a U-boat commander decide that a torpedo was a better bet after all. However, he had to be philosophical about it; he'd been given no choice – in the navy you obeyed orders and that was that. He supposed it was a compliment in a way; but one that had two sides to it.

Three days later his appointment came through in the Commission and Warrant List: he was appointed in the rank of lieutenant to HMS *Nonsuch* for disposal – that word again. A check on the Navy List showed that *Nonsuch* was a shore establishment, a naval establishment in the commercial port of Cardiff in South Wales. Since the Captain in the barracks had by inference intended a sea appointment, Tom, becoming accustomed to naval ways and terms, deduced that *Nonsuch* was a base, or headquarters – perhaps Commander Gordon Campbell's HQ – from which officers and ratings were 'disposed' to seagoing ships. At any rate, he hoped so.

Meanwhile he had leave. He was to report to *Nonsuch* in seven days' time. His steward packed his gear, the paymaster's office provided him with a first-class travel warrant, he took his leave of the shouts and screams of the gunners' mates, the tramp of ever-marching feet and the clang of metal parts as the big guns were laboriously stripped down and reassembled, and took the train from the Harbour railway station to Waterloo. He made his way to Euston for the train north and the night ferry leaving Liverpool for

Dublin's North Wall. It would be good to see his home again.

He had not communicated with Grace Handley. It would seem pointless really . . . but he left Portsmouth with a number of regrets and whilst aboard the ferry he scribbled a note, which he posted in Dublin, giving her his address, HMS *Nonsuch*. When his sea appointment came through, *Nonsuch* would forward mail, readdressed as was customary to his ship c/o GPO, London.

FIVE

HIS FATHER HAD AGED; HE DODDERED now, pottering around the house somewhat aimlessly and seldom venturing into the garden lying bleakly beneath the west of Ireland's winter skies with the wind blustering in from the Atlantic. Tom had a strong feeling that the deanery of Moyna would not be his home for much longer. Tom's brothers agreed. It so happened that both were there on Tom's arrival from the railway station at Galway City from Dublin's Westland Row: Philip, on leave from his regiment serving in the Flanders mud, and Edward taking a sabbatical from his duties as a parson of the Church of Ireland.

'He's really past it,' Edward said, shaking his head. 'Indeed the Bishop's most concerned, *most* concerned.' He looked at Tom over fingertips placed devoutly together. 'Anyone of Father's age . . . to be dispossessed of his home. It's tragic. The Bishop naturally recognizes that, but what can he do? I think his hope is that Father will resign.'

'He can't afford to,' Tom pointed out. The family was as poor as a church mouse, relatively. 'What would happen to him if he left the deanery? He'd disintegrate, leaving behind all his memories of the old days, and Mother . . . and – and all of that,' he ended lamely.

'The real point is, where would he live?' Philip asked. He looked quizzically at Edward. 'Of course, your rectory's large enough, I suppose.'

Edward's lips set. He looked unhappy; he knew that neither Tom nor Philip had homes that could shelter an old man growing into senility. 'Well, yes,' he conceded cautiously. 'Large enough but there are problems, as you know. Edith is not strong, and Father tends to tire her. I feel it would be scarcely fair to ask her to cope. No, I don't see that as the answer.'

So much for Christian charity, Tom thought. Everything, he remembered, had always been too much for Edith, who had the aspect of a piece of wet string. Currently, she was upstairs with a headache. Bugger Edith. A room with a landlady in Galway City was likely to be the Dean's fate, where he would spend his lonely days with his memories and an occasional walk down to the Claddagh to watch the rollers coming past the Aran Islands into Galway Bay . . .

Philip changed the subject, spoke of the conditions on the Western Front, of the everlasting mud, the rats, the squalor of the dugouts, the horrifying casualties of the Marne but also, with a kind of wonder, of the cheerfulness and sheer courage of the troops who faced the dangers and the privations with no more than the routine barrack-room grumbling.

'You're lucky to be in the navy, Tom. Always a bath at hand, clean clothes, always a meal.' He passed his cigarette-case; Tom took one and lit up. Edward, with a grimace of disapproval, refused. Philip laughed. 'Always the cleric. I'll tell you something: if it wasn't for a fag, we'd have lost heart weeks ago. A fag's a solace, something to be looked forward to, the first thing you do for a wounded man – shove a fag in his mouth. Fags and women,' he said with a sideways look at Edward's frown. 'When there are any, that is. Back behind the lines when your turn comes to be relieved. What about you, Tom? Girl in every port – or what?'

Tom shrugged. 'Hardly. Not much time for that sort of thing.'

'Oh, come on! Time can always be made. And it's time you got married, old son.' Philip had been married some years earlier; his wife had died in childbirth; the baby, a boy, had not survived. He had not married again. Tom murmured something about not wishing to marry while the war lasted.

'Oh, so there is someone?'

Tom said, 'I haven't said so. How do you make that out?'

'Just the way you said it, Tom.'

'Well . . . no, there isn't. Not since Dolores –'

'The Argentinian?'

'Yes.'

'Father,' Edward said solemnly, 'was *delighted* when that came to an end, I can tell you.'

Tom snapped, 'It wasn't Father's business. Or yours, Edward, come to that.' Suddenly he had a strong desire to wipe away the prim look of sanctity on his brother's face, horse-like above the clerical collar and black stock. He exaggerated, deliberately. 'As a matter of fact there is someone. But it would mean a divorce if it was to come to anything.'

The startled jump that Edward gave was quite gratifying. But later Tom regretted the impulse that had led to indiscretion. A day or two later he was sitting on a garden bench not far from the Dean's study window, which was open to admit the fresh air of a bright, sunny day with a welcome absence of any wind, when he became aware of a conversation between brother Edward and his father. 'I've never heard such a monstrous thing, Edward! To bring the scandal of divorce into a clerical family! As you say, the woman's very obviously a Bad Lot.' The capital letters could be heard distinctly. The Dean's voice took on a pathetic note. 'It's so *dreadfully* unfair . . . at my age. So many worries.' The Dean, with the facility of old age, went on to something else. 'These wretched Fenians. Causing havoc in Dublin, I hear. Attacking our troops – demanding Home Rule – all in the middle of a war. Even here in Moyna as you know. An RIC constable killed only the other day. Shot down like a rabbit . . .'

At the end of his leave Tom went back to duty worrying about his father and the wrong impression he'd been given of Grace Handley and, by the same token, of Tom himself. It was not a matter that could be put right, and his father had never in fact taxed him with it. Tom's hope was that he'd forgotten already.

HMS *Nonsuch* turned out to be a commandeered hotel, a former temperance hotel not far from the railway station in Cardiff. Tom went in uniform past an armed sentry who gave him a smart butt salute. He gave his name to a petty officer in a cubicle just inside the door. He was expected.

'Room 104, sir. Up the stairs and turn right, sir.'

The building was busy with naval personnel, officers and ratings, RN and reserves, hurrying about looking preoccupied. Tom wondered what their various missions might be; and reflected on something he'd been told in a friendly off-parade conversation with the course gunner's mate at Whale Island. 'There was this man, sir, in the barracks. Proper skiver till 'e was bowled out. Told the Commodore straight at Defaulters. Found out somehow that 'is name had never appeared on any of the drafting master-at-arms' lists. Used to fall in on the parade-ground when Both Watches was piped at 0800 each day. Fell out with the special parties when they was dismissed as is the routine, sir. Picked up a plank that 'e'd stowed somewhere the afternoon before, walked round the bloody place with it every time an officer or PO came in sight, never got picked up because 'e looked *busy*, see? Never did a hand's turn and never got drafted to sea. You get some like that, sir,' the PO added gloomily but philosophically.

Tom had asked how the man got picked up in the end.

'Returned aboard drunk, sir. Very drunk, attempted to strike the crusher,' he said, in reference to the master-at-arms' deputy, the regulating petty officer, known from time immemorial as the crusher on account of the number of cockroaches slaughtered by the traditionally big feet of the ship's police.

Some of these busy-looking officers and ratings, the latter mostly writers of the accountant branch, carried sheaves of papers. The equivalent of the plank?

This time there was no brassbound Captain. An assistant paymaster, white cloth between the two gold stripes of his rank, gave him his orders.

The paymaster scanned a list. 'Lieutenant Chatto . . . to join *Thornton* as watchkeeper and navigating officer. She's lying in Barry Dock, that's just down the line from Cardiff General.'

'Any other information?'

The paymaster grinned happily. It wasn't he who had to go to sea in what Tom was to find was a tramp steamer, a collier, filthy with coal-dust. 'You'll find out, old man,' was all the paymaster would say. There wouldn't be any mention of Q ships.

The port of Barry was, with Cardiff and Swansea, one of the busiest of Britain's coal-loading ports. The South Wales pits produced the best coal possible for the use of ships' boilers. Few engineers, RN or merchant service, would gladly accept anything else. Thus South Wales coal went out from Barry Dock to all the world's overseas coaling stations from Gibraltar round the globe to Valparaiso and back again. Welsh coal had always been used by the liners of the PSNC; but never had Tom thought he would end up in the dreary place from whence it came, still less find himself transferred from the clean, hosed-down decks of a liner to the indescribable mess that he found aboard the *Thornton* lying in the basin at Barry Dock.

And it had to stay like that, he was told. Reporting aboard, he was taken by a somewhat dirty individual to be introduced to the Captain, who was equally dirty and wore a disreputable blue serge suit. The Captain, who turned out to be a lieutenant-commander RN, grinned at Tom's face and gave his first order.

'I take it you've brought civilian clothes, Chatto?'

'Yes, sir –'

'Dirty?'

'Well, no –'

'Dirty 'em up, Chatto. And get out of that fancy uniform double quick. Silly buggers at *Nonsuch* should have told you not to join in uniform. You're Second Mate of a collier now – so far as the rest of the world's concerned. I'll pass the word that an officer boarded to check papers or something – just in case the Kaiser's long ears reach Barry.'

'And when I'm not seen to go ashore, sir?'

'Oh, we'll cross that bridge if we come to it. I'll say we ate you for dinner. We have that sort of reputation, you know.' He added, 'Mind you, Chatto, all this secrecy is a simple case of BBB.'

'BBB?'

'Bullshit Baffles Brains. I'd bet a month's pay that Little Willy knows all about Q ships by now. But you still don't breathe a word.' The Captain somewhat belatedly reached out a large hand and shook Tom's. 'Anyway – welcome aboard! We can do with you. You're going to be kept busy. As well as navigator, you're going to be my gunnery officer.'

Tom was dismayed and looked it. The Captain, whose name was Fletcher, laughed. 'You don't imagine Whale Island was all for nowt, do you? The service always gets its pound of flesh, but don't worry, you'll have a gunlayer, a leading hand who knows his job backwards, good as any gunner's mate.'

'I'm glad to hear that, sir.'

Fletcher nodded and went on, 'You'll find us a happy bunch. Unorthodox and happy. And we've a real job to do, make no mistake about that. By the way, the chap who brought you in just now. What did you think he was? Be honest.'

Tom answered cautiously. 'I really don't know, sir. But from what you've said . . . I imagine he was an officer?'

'Dead right! Sub-Lieutenant Lasenby, Royal Navy. Newly promoted. Last appointment senior midshipman in the *Collingwood.* Like you, he's undergoing a sea change. I understand you come from the liners?'

'Yes –'

'This is rather different.' Fletcher grinned. 'The people who sail the tramp ships are not very pukka. Good seamen, but what an aunt of mine would call Not Quite, if that. But seriously, Chatto, this is something new for the navy and we've got to make a success of it. For the country's sake . . . The naval high command is staking a lot on our results, us and the other Q ships.' He looked at a brass-rimmed clock on the cabin bulkhead. 'Go along and make yourself at home, Chatto. We leave for Gibraltar at three bells in the first dog. That's for fitting-out and being equipped with our guns. Also a change of name.'

'Change of anything else, sir?' Tom asked, tongue in cheek.

'What? Oh. No. We'll still be dirty!'

Leading Seaman Tubbs, a three-badge fleet reservist who had opened a greengrocer's shop in his home depot of Devonport, when placed four years earlier on the time-expired reserve list, had looked with a degree of desperation at what were to be his gun's crews when the collier went into action against German submarines. In the absence of the guns yet to be fitted, he had lectured his ratings on what was going to be expected of them. And the lecturing had caused the start of his despair. All young, mostly signed on as Hostilities Only men for the duration of the war, they looked to him unpromising. Dressed in civvies as per orders, they looked thoroughly scruffy, but maybe that wasn't their fault. That apart, they all seemed bewildered by war after short training courses at the barracks in Pompey, Guz or Chats. Leading Seaman Tubbs told them a home truth or two.

'Thicker'n my bleedin' cabbages of yore, you are. I just wish I was back with me sprouts and onions . . . to say nothing of me old lady who'll sure as eggs is eggs bugger up the whole show in me absence defending 'Is Majesty the King and trying to drum summat into you perishin' lot.' He sighed. 'God give me strength to survive. Now bloody *listen*, right? Up the straits, that's to say in Gibraltar for those as don't know, we'll be fitted with two 4.7-inch guns and two 12-pounders, plus machine-guns mounted in the bridge wings. The 4.7s, they'll be one each side. Port and starboard, and don't go an' forget which is which, right? Now, them two guns, they'll be mounted behind gunport doors what are yet to be carved out o' the ship's sides by the dockyard mateys in Gib. They'll be hinged flaps like, the outboard side lying flush with the ship's plates so the enemy don't see any difference, see? The inboard sides, they'll be painted with a bloody great Union flag. When orders come from the skipper or the gunnery officer, them flaps are opened up and the gun on the attack side is run out into its firing position. At the same time, the yeoman on the bridge whips down the Red Ensign and runs up the battle ensign, the White Ensign o' the British Navy. Thus, see, we don't open fire under false colours, right?'

There was a query. 'Why's that, killick?' Leading hands were known as killicks on account of the anchor worn as rank insignia on the left upper arm above the good conduct chevrons. 'Why not just open fire like?'

'Don't ask me, lad,' Tubbs said crossly. 'That's for the officers, not the likes o' me an' you. But I reckon it's to do with some sort o' international bullshit, Parliament an' that. Them buggers like things done proper so they don't get the backlash. Only principle the fuckers know is, keep your own nose clean, square your own yardarm, or as more commonly said, never crap on your own doorstep. Get me, do you?'

They did, apparently. Tubbs went on, 'We're getting a rocky – that's RNR, rocky stripes, see – as the gunnery bloke. Don't know yet 'ow much 'e knows, but me, I been a gunnery rate for more years than I bloody remember. Short-course officers . . . I was told once by Windy Pantlin, Chief PO wot was chief gunner's mate o' the parade in Guz . . . said to me, 'e did, that when 'e was an instructor at the gunnery school, the commander didn't go much on failures, so they made sure they all passed out. Gunner's mate used to 'old up a gun part and ask, "If I said this was the catch retaining breech-block open, sir, would you say I was right?" Things like that. Well, I ask you! That's not to say our bloke won't turn out good, o' course.'

Petty Officer Brewster, chief boatswain's mate-to-be of the *Thornton*, was an active service rating, which was to say that he was not time-expired and had not gone on the reserve. Brewster was cynical about the fleet reserve men. Ancient sea-daddies some of them, not to say sea-grand-daddies in many cases, men who were past it, crusted Barnacle Bills who looked as though they had last gone to sea back in the days of Rear-Admiral the Earl of Clanwilliam in the Sail Training Squadron. Shellbacks who would be lost in the modern navy of Lord Fisher, the navy of the up-and-coming men like Jellicoe and Beatty.

Also, Petty Officer Brewster was a Yorkshire tyke, born in Leeds but now from Masham on the fringe of Wensleydale, he having married a Masham girl. As a Yorkshireman, he was sceptical of anyone who was not a Yorkshireman. In Yorkshire, as well as sturdy dales farmers, they bred the best seamen, starting back in history with Captain Cook of Whitby. During his naval career, Petty Officer Brewster had had many an argument, and many a fight too, with those who didn't appreciate his abrasiveness. Being a Yorkshire-man, he had always won. He didn't in fact argue; he stated. And that was that.

He had been on leave when his draft chit had been put through in Pompey barracks; he had a mate in the drafting master-at-arms' office and this mate had sent him a telegram of warning. There was no recall from leave, but his friend thought he might like to know what awaited him on his return. But in fact all the telegram said was the one word: *Barry*. Security would permit of no more, so really it wasn't very helpful. Brewster scratched his head. 'Barry, that's in South Wales. Bloody coal port! Now what's int' wind, eh?' He felt irritated, and turned on his wife. 'Don't just stand there, lass. Put t'kettle on and look lively.'

The kettle, black and solid, went on the kitchen range. 'What's in the telegram, Bob?'

'Draft, looks like.'

'Sea?'

'How the soddin' hell do I know, eh? It's bloody cryptic, that's what it is. Barry! Could be a TBD, I s'pose, but I dunno.' Brewster was worried; Barry had an ominous sound, somehow, something out of routine. Brewster liked routine, the routine of a battleship or an armoured cruiser, with literally hundreds of pusser seamen for weight to be chucked at and officers who always backed their senior ratings right or wrong, though Brewster himself was never wrong. He chewed it over disconsolately for the remainder of his leave and the night before taking the carrier's motor-bus to Ripon for York and the railway journey south, he took his wife Maisie for a farewell drink in the snug of the Black Bull off the market square before detailing her off for the conduct of his home in his absence.

'Old Peculier,' he said to the landlord. 'Pint.'

'And the missus?'

'Well – not Old Peculier any road. Goes to 'er 'ead. 'Alf of cider. Packet o' nuts. Small one.'

The order was passed across. The landlord was sardonic. 'Celebrating, are we?'

Brewster glared. He didn't like familiarity. 'Doan't know

about you. I'm not.' Then he added importantly, 'Away tomorrow, kitbag an' 'ammick.'

'Back to sea?' the landlord asked, busy polishing glasses.

'Probably. Can't say. Got to be circumspect.' That was a good word.

The landlord peered around the cheerful friendliness of the snug. 'Doan't see no Kaiser.'

'I'll thank you not to be passing opinions when they're not asked,' Brewster said, and carried his order across to Maisie. Maisie was younger than himself, and good-looking. Brewster caught the smirk on her face as she exchanged glances across the bar with a middle-aged farmer sitting alone in the public over a pint of Theakston's best bitter. Petty Officer Brewster's temper rose, but he wasn't going to make a scene in the Black Bull. He waited until they were on their way back to his cottage in the lee of Theakston's brewery. 'You can cut that out, lass,' he said savagely. 'I saw you looking at that yokel. When I'm gone . . . just remember. Serving King and country is what I'll be doing. You carry on like that and I'll take my belt to you soon as I get back.'

Maisie answered submissively. It didn't do to anger Bob. When they got indoors, the orders were given: mind and keep the place clean, sweep and polish, buff up the brass like aboard a ship, petty officers didn't live in cowdung conditions, tan the children if they got uppity with Dad away again, make sure she went to church regular while he was at sea, but don't put more than a penny in the collection, there was no need for extravagance and the perishing church was loaded to the main deck with cash. And brass was brass.

Two days later, in a filthy and pervading drizzle, Petty Officer Brewster, in plain clothes brought from his locker in the POs' mess as ordered by the drafting master-at-arms in Portsmouth barracks and accompanied by his kitbag and hammock, stood gazing up at the decks of his new ship. On the bridge was a person dressed in a scruffy blue serge suit and wearing a bowler hat. He was probably a dockyard foreman.

This person caught sight of the lurking Brewster. He called down to the jetty. 'You there. Are you joining the ship, or just gawping?'

Dockyard foremen didn't have that sort of voice. Petty Officer Brewster jumped to attention. 'Yessir. Sorry, sir. Coming aboard to join, sir.'

This was before Tom had joined the ship. By the time he did so, the full complement was aboard. The upper-deck ratings consisted of thirty-five able seamen and ordinary seamen, four leading hands, two petty officers – Brewster and a fleet reservist named Popplewell, a shellback according to Brewster. These would form the guns' crews and boarding parties as well as part-of-ship hands. The bridge staff included a leading signalman, also a fleet reservist, and two signalmen first-class. The engine-room was manned by eighteen stokers, three leading stokers, a stoker petty officer, three engine-room artificers first-class with a warrant engineer RN in overall charge. The ship's company was completed by two officers' stewards, two telegraphists, a cook under a leading cook, and one supply assistant. The small wardroom consisted of the First Lieutenant, an RNR like Tom, named Stallybrass; two RNVR lieutenants, plus Sub-Lieutenant Lasenby (who also happened to be a Yorkshireman) and a surgeon probationer, Dr Grant-Wylie, recently qualified from St Thomas's Hospital in London. He gave Tom the impression of being scared out of his wits both at being aboard a ship and at having in future to make unaided diagnoses. Fletcher had reassured him.

'It'll be mostly VD, Doctor.'

Dr Grant-Wylie had, it seemed, been mugging up on the various regulations regarding disease control. He was mindful of the Contagious Diseases Act. 'Have we a CDA mess aboard, sir?'

'No. Because so far we haven't any VD cases. Or I hope we haven't. So far we haven't had a doctor either. If the occasion arises, I'll cross that bridge, not that we've a lot of space to spare.' This was very evident: the ship's company, under war conditions and in preparation for their future role, was very much larger than would normally be carried by a tramp ship.

Before the ship's company went to their stations for leaving harbour, the First Lieutenant passed the order to clear lower deck, and for the hands to muster, not on the open deck, but in the seclusion of the engineers' alleyway which was just big enough to take men packed in like sardines. When the First Lieutenant reported the ship's company present and correct, Fletcher went below to address them. He was brief and to the point.

'As most of you know already, we leave for Gibraltar at 1730. Our conversion will take place in the dockyard there. Now – we may be small, we may be filthy. We may not be the *Iron Duke* or the *Lion*, but we'll be packing enough gun power to sink any German submarines that show themselves. That's our job: to be a decoy. Once our guns are fitted, the guns' crews will be exercised again and again until we're an efficient fighting unit – and after that, we'll go on exercising down to stopwatch precision, speed being of the essence once we have a surfaced U-boat in our sights.' He paused, running his gaze down the lines of men. 'We'll be a motley collection to the prying eye, and that's what we want. It's our orders to be scruffy at all times on deck. We're a tramp crew and we don't have fancy uniforms or fancy manners. But that does not excuse slovenliness below and it does not imply any relaxation of proper naval discipline internally. The Articles of War and the Naval Discipline Act hold good aboard us just as much as in the main battle fleets at sea. I trust that is quite clearly understood.' He glanced at the First Lieutenant. 'Carry on, if you please, Number One.'

Lieutenant Stallybrass dismissed the hands. Fifty minutes

later half-a-dozen seamen mustered in dribs and drabs on the fo'c'sle-head and poop to stand by to let go the wires and ropes when the order came from the bridge. Moving for'ard and aft at speed, keeping an eye on the unberthing parties, Petty Officer Brewster, chief boatswain's mate and well aware of it, looked with distaste at the curious assortment of rigs: corduroy trousers, canvas trousers, collarless shirts, belts and braces, cloth caps . . . he himself was little better, as he had to admit, but at least he wore a collar, a starched one, and he was *clean*. He reflected that he had no doubt been given this draft in order to act as ramrod. Well – ramrod he would be. And it was always better to start as you meant to go on. He started; he picked on a young ordinary seaman who was standing back hesitantly from the wire leading from the ship's bitts, through the fairlead, to the shore bollard.

'You there, that man! Forget your lilywhite hands, right? I don't like skulkers – grab a hold –'

He broke off. A quiet but authoritative voice was coming down upon him from the bridge. From the Captain, in his blue serge and bowler hat. And no collar. 'Can it, Whack. Bloke's doing 'is bleedin' best. Give 'im a chance, Whack.'

Whack. Uttered twice. Stone the bloody crows. Petty Officer Brewster felt poleaxed and his face went a very deep red. *Whack!* It was perhaps just as well he'd heard that word in time to inhibit what would have been his normal reaction to a shout from the bridge: coming to attention and saluting the Captain. He swallowed hard; but he had to come to terms with the orders issued by Their Lordships in their wisdom. At the same time he was going to score a point of his own, as would any proud Yorkshireman. He waved a hand towards the bridge.

'Righto, skip,' he said. That would teach him . . . but it didn't seem to. Fletcher looked pleased, smiling approvingly.

With Petty Officer Brewster muttering angrily to himself, the *Thornton* passed through the lock and headed out into Barry Roads.

SIX

PASSING OUT OF THE BRISTOL CHANNEL to head south for Cape Cornwall and the Longships Light, the *Thornton* met deteriorating weather and the beginning of the North Atlantic swell. The cold was intense on the open deck; some light snow had started falling and the bridge watchkeepers were huddled into greatcoats, oilskins and sou'westers. Below, there was a cold fug. Grime was everywhere; the ship's cargo holds had not been cleaned out, and coal-dust was a pervasive thing. With empty holds, the ship heaved around badly in the swell. Many of the lower-deck men were going to sea for the first time, and there was a good deal of seasickness to add to the stench and squalor. There was no appeal for medical help. Dr Grant-Wylie was seasick too, unable to leave the bunk in his tiny cabin.

Two nights later, in the turbulent waters of the Bay of Biscay, Tom had the middle watch, the graveyard watch as seamen know it. At two bells Fletcher climbed the ladder and came up alongside him. 'Couldn't sleep,' he said abruptly. 'Must be the galley.' The evening meal in the wardroom had been rissoles, done to a cinder. Probably the meal served to the Captain in his cabin had been no better. Fletcher looked ahead through his binoculars, then scanned all around the horizons. There was a lot of low cloud and the visibility was poor. Fletcher remarked on this. 'You're checking on the lookouts, of course?'

'Yes, sir. They're all right when they're not being sick. They've a concern for their own lives.'

Fletcher nodded. 'Our first line of defence!'

'Our *only* line of defence till we get our guns.'

'Right. I argued the toss with *Nonsuch*, and with the Admiralty too. Why not fit us out in a home port? The answer was the usual one – too busy with the heavy stuff.' Fletcher looked again through his binoculars, felt the steady thump of the old tramp's engines as they turned her single shaft and its screw. The steadiness was a reassurance: the engines at all events had been well looked after. Fletcher's warrant engineer had given a good report of them after his first inspection.

Fletcher lowered his glasses. He moved from the bridge wing into the wheelhouse, checked the barometer, which was falling. He cursed to himself; that barometer was about the only aid the ship possessed. No power-steering, no gyro compass, only magnetic which meant the working out of sums each time course was altered, taking into account the deviation and variation which changed with every degree of shift; the barometer and the engine-room telegraph, that was about the lot.

He had a word with the helmsman. 'All well, Barrett?'

'Aye, sir. All's well.'

'You're an active service rating, aren't you?'

'Yes, sir. Due to go out on pension, I was, sir, day before the war started.'

'Bad luck – or was it?' There were plenty of men who didn't want to take their pensions, the navy had become a way of life.

Barrett said, 'Not really bad luck, sir, no.' His tone was flat, unemotional, controlled. Fletcher had had some years' experience of seamen. As a Divisional Lieutenant in a battle-cruiser he had dealt with many of the aspects of the seamen's lives, both service and private. Advancements, requests for leave or for qualifying courses in gunnery, torpedoes and so on – and their family concerns as well, since a Divisional Officer was expected to be guide, counseller and friend on appropriate occasions. And there had been something in the way Able Seaman Barrett had answered that raised a doubt. Problems at home, problems that he didn't wish to face – marital probably? That was usually the trouble. Men had so many long absences from home. Two years with the Mediterranean Fleet, three years with the China Squadron . . . it was hard on the womenfolk. Fletcher dismissed it from his mind as he went back to join Tom Chatto in the starboard wing. He didn't relish the thought of shoreside worries distracting his ship's company in wartime but it was inevitable, and perhaps Barrett would put in a request to see him if he wanted to talk about it one day.

He stood for a moment with Tom, who was continuing the constantly needed binocular scan of the sea's surface, watching for the feather of water – not easy in the confused swell – that would indicate a periscope; watching for the heave of water followed by the squat shape that would become the conning-tower of a surfacing U-boat. Maintaining vigilance was all that could be done. And after that a fast reaction if the enemy should materialize out of the depths. And after that, what? There was only one answer: run for it – and pray. So far without guns, they would be as helpless as any merchant ship in dangerous waters. Somebody at the Admiralty, Tom thought, needed his head read.

He paced the bridge, from wing to wing through the wheelhouse as Fletcher went back below to his cabin beneath the bridge and chartroom. The feel of the collier beneath him was very different from that of the liners of PSNC, well-found ships with tried and efficient crews. The liner deck-hands . . . good seamen all of them. Tom thought for a moment of Petty Officer Brewster; he had encountered the chief boatswain's mate – or buffer, as such were commonly known in the service – only briefly in the short time since he had joined the ship, but he had formed an impression of a man steeped in bull, a self-important man who could prove an irritant to the hands. In Tom's as yet short experience of the navy, Brewster's nearest equivalents were the gunners' mates at Whale Island, and all were worlds apart from their merchant-ship counterpart, the boatswain. Most of the senior deck ratings in the liners were pure seamen to their fingertips, steeped in the ocean, and virtually all of them were still, as it were, filched from the windjammers. With few exceptions, they had little flannel and did not chuck their weight around unnecessarily. Brewster had the sound of a potential bully . . .

For the hundredth time Tom brought up his binoculars, carrying out yet another broad sweep. His glasses fixed on something: he didn't know what, it was too vague in the night. He knew from long sea experience that the eyes could play tricks after much use of binoculars, and the more so at night. He used the seaman's habit of looking to one side of the object, if it was an object, rather than directly at it.

Still vague. Tom spoke to the bridge lookout. 'Two points on the port bow, Williams. See anything?'

'Dunno, sir.' Williams examined the bearing closely. 'I reckon it's nothing, sir.'

Not definite enough, certainly, to be a surfacing submarine, not even a periscope lifted to just above the surface. Then, just some half-minute later, a bright shaft of moonlight broke through the overcast and lit on something. Not, however, on the bearing that had aroused Tom's suspicions: dead ahead of their track, the lethal horn of a mine.

Speed, now. And no time to call the Captain first. Tom ran for the wheelhouse, wrenched the engine-room telegraph to emergency full astern and ordered the wheel hard over to starboard. Fletcher, still awake, felt the helm and engine movements. He was on the bridge within half a minute. Tom reported, 'Mine dead ahead, sir!'

'Right. Sound the alarm, Chatto.'

Tom ran for the alarm button, one of the *Thornton*'s few modern contrivances, an electrically-operated alarm system that would sound throughout the ship. As the strident rattle broke out Fletcher saw for himself the action Tom had already taken. 'Good lad,' he said approvingly. Bringing up his binoculars he found the mine now on their starboard side, brought there by Tom's prompt action in putting the helm to starboard so that the ship swung to port. The days were yet far ahead when the connections between wheel and rudderhead would be crossed so that starboard wheel would also mean starboard turn. Fletcher said, 'The bugger's floating . . . must have broken away from its sinker somewhere. I doubt if we've strayed into a minefield, and thank God for that at all events.'

He used the voice-pipe to the starting-platform in the engine-room. The warrant engineer answered.

'Chief – we've raised a floating mine. Stand by for a bang.'

'Likely to hit, sir?'

'Not if I can help it! I'll blow it by rifle-fire. Can't leave it as a danger to other shipping.' Fletcher slammed back the voice-pipe cover.

Mr Wenstock, warrant engineer, wiped his streaming forehead with a fistful of cotton-waste. He looked sour; he felt it. He was a martyr to indigestion and the rissoles hadn't helped. He listened to the thump and rattle of his engines and drew some comfort from them. Reciprocating engines, they were, with huge steel pistons that rose and fell as they turned the single shaft. Old, but good yet. And like all things old, they were reliable. Mr Wenstock always grew sentimental about his engines, the space where he was king for a while, at any rate in a ship, like this one, where there was no commissioned engineer officer to steal the glory. And it hadn't taken him long to get sentimental about these old beauties that had gallantly done their job for so very many uncomplaining years of hard slog at sea. And he hoped, now, that they weren't about to die by outside interference. The bloody Kaiser and his mines – though, of course, seeing as how it had broken adrift from its sinker, it could be British. Sod it, anyhow. Mines . . . an old mate of Mr Wenstock's had bought it from a mine when one had bumped the side of his light cruiser, slap against the engine-room. Mr Wenstock had never in fact seen an engine-room blow up, but he had an imagination and he could visualize the super-heated steam from fractured pipes searing the flesh off the stokers and ERAs, and the flame and roar of the explosion and then the consuming fire until the sea came pouring in. No one could live through that. There would have been nothing left of his mate except maybe bloody strips of burnt flesh.

And any mine could do that. Even if it was British. Mr Wenstock began to pray. As ever, the poor bloody engine-room complement was wholly in the hands of the executive officers on the bridge. And some were better at their jobs than others.

'You and you and you. Get a soddin' move on, smack it about or I'll be having your guts for garters and your balls for breakfast.' Petty Officer Brewster had his chance now to be a ramrod. He'd drawn the keys of the rifle stowage – thank God the Admiralty had had *some* sense – and had issued arms to three of his as yet untried hands, one of them being Leading Seaman Tubbs. He'd had harsh words with Tubbs, who'd considered it his job as a gunnery rate to have charge of the keys, but he'd slapped Tubbs down firmly, thus making an enemy but he didn't care.

The ratings armed, Brewster marched them to the fore well-deck. He halted them, then looked around: he saw the mine not so far off the starboard side. A little too close for comfort. He saw the Captain on the starboard side of the fo'c'sle. Well, they were at sea, it was night, even if there was light from the moon, and there were no spies around, so he could be as pusser as he liked. It would do the Hostilities Only ratings good to see how things were done proper.

'Party, stand at ease . . . stand easy. Look out for them perishin' rifles, they're not toy guns bought by mummy for Christmas.' Standing at attention, noting the angry look on

Tubbs' face, he turned for'ard and brought his hand to the salute before remembering he was wearing a cloth cap.

'Chief boatswain's mate, sir, reporting mine firing party present and correct. Sir.'

Fletcher looked down from the fo'c'sle, feeling irritated by the PO's unnecessary parade-ground stance. 'Thank you, Petty Officer Brewster.' Not Whack – thank goodness. 'The mine's too close at the moment. Get the hands in the lee of the fo'c'sle, and stand by.'

'Yessir,' Brewster said briskly. 'Party, atten. . .*tion*! Turn for'ard, dis. . .miss.' A pause, then another shout. 'Fall in again, lee o' the fo'c'sle as ordered. Look sharp, don't slouch, keep awake, and *mind them rifles*!' One of the HO men had got his rifle somehow stuck between his legs and had nearly fallen over. Brewster heard something he wasn't meant to hear: the Captain, not quite *sotto voce* . . . something uncomplimentary, which annoyed Brewster but there was nothing he could do about it. Not, at any rate, while he was not being Whack . . .

To score a hit on a floating mine at night was not easy. With the exception of Leading Seaman Tubbs the ratings were far from being experienced shots, having fired only one clip of cartridges each whilst at their basic training establishments; and Tubbs happened to have a finger in a heavy bandage owing to a mishap when returning from shore leave the night before sailing. Damaged finger, and a black eye. The Welsh hadn't liked having fun poked at them by an Englishman, one of a lower order of citizenry by their standards. It was not his trigger finger, but it didn't help.

Petty Officer Brewster gave instructions. 'No good just blasting orf at it in 'opes like. You got to aim for the 'orns. It's them as ignites the primer.'

Not so easy at all. The mine spun and lolled, the horns kept moving under and up again, then under again. On the bridge Tom used a megaphone and called out to Fletcher on the fo'c'sle-head. 'It seems as if it's chasing us, sir. It seems to answer every helm and engine movement. I think we'll have to take a chance, blow it while we can.'

Fletcher waved back but didn't comment. Everyone on deck was watching the mine. Very suddenly it was lifted by a heavier-than-usual swell. It rose to the crest, teetered for a long moment of horror, then swooped down the side of the wave, making direct for the collier's side aft. Tom reacted fast. He ordered the helm hard over and called the engine-room. 'Everything you've got, Chief . . . even if you shear the holding-down bolts!'

Now it was really a case of touch-and-go. As the ship's head moved away, and as the extra power on the engines had some effect, the watching men all seemed to hold their breath. They all knew what might happen, literally at any moment. In the instant that one of the horns impacted against the ship's side it would be the end and they would all become names in the casualty lists and in the telegrams to their families. Nails dug into palms. Fletcher was ready to order abandon ship the moment the explosion came – if he was still alive, which would be doubtful, and if there was any ship left to abandon. Nevertheless the naval mind worked along set routes: you always had your orders ready. For similar reasons Petty Officer Popplewell, while Brewster was occupied with his riflemen, had mustered a lowering party and had got the seaboat swung out on the falls and ready to be put in the water.

Nearer and nearer; then momentarily stayed by another freak swell coming beneath the collier's bottom. Much too close now for the rifles to be used. But the mine appeared to be drawing aft.

It echoed right through the engine-room. Everything shook and clanged and rattled. The giant pistons seemed to Mr Wenstock almost to jump from their beds. There was a smell of high explosive coming down the ventilation shafts. There was something in the air that seemed to stifle.

But the engine-room was, amazingly, still there, as was Mr Wenstock and his black gang. The pistons resumed their up-and-down movement, nonchalantly, as though nothing at all had happened other than some temporary aberration.

Then the voice-pipe from the bridge whistled at Mr Wenstock. He lifted the cover with a shaking hand. 'Chief here,' he said.

It was Fletcher. 'All over, Chief. Mine blown. Resume normal cruising stations. And well done, Chief. If it hadn't been for fast responses from the engine-room, and equally on the bridge . . . that would have been the end even before we've started.'

Mr Wenstock was pleased to be complimented; it was a good mark for those old reciprocating engines, those pistons tirelessly thundering up and down. But normal cruising stations . . . until this war ended, nothing was going to be normal. Mr Wenstock much regretted the ending of the peace-time routines. Not because he was scared – although from time to time, like tonight, he *would* be scared – but rather on account of his wife back in Pompey. She had looked forward to his retirement, which hadn't been long ahead. Now, God knew when he'd be seeing Pompey again: and Edna wasn't well, not well at all. She'd been in and out of the Portsmouth Royal Hospital over the past eighteen months and they didn't seem to know what was up with her.

After that long night the weather improved. The *Thornton* made good progress south, the lookouts and Officers of the Watch remaining vigilant as the old collier came out of the Bay of Biscay past Cape Finisterre. During the morning watch after the mine episode, Leading Seaman Tubbs had a word with Petty Officer Brewster. He hadn't liked the way he'd been treated to a lecture on how to open fire on a floating mine.

'I'm not a newly joined OD,' he said. 'Leading 'and, *and* a non-sub rating as gunlayer first-class.' He sniffed; Brewster's non-sub rate was no more than seaman gunner. 'Just thought I'd mention it, like.'

Brewster snorted. He laid a hand on Tubbs' left upper arm where, had he been wearing uniform, the anchor of his rate would have been along with his three good conduct badges. 'Watch it,' he said in his rather grating voice. 'Killicks can be lost, Leading Seaman Tubbs, due to insubordination or insolence. I don't take cheek from anyone.'

Tubbs flushed and protested. 'Didn't mean no insolence, PO. I – just –'

'I said, watch it.' Brewster turned away and marched along the deck, arms swinging. Out of uniform, in an old pair of brown trousers and a shabby waistcoat, Tubbs thought he looked a proper charlie.

Brewster's voice had been, as usual, loud; the conversation had taken place outside Tom's cabin port. Tom's mind was too full of last night's episode for him to find sleep. He made a mental note. As gunnery officer, Leading Seaman Tubbs would be one of his personnel responsibilities. Tubbs was a decent sort, chubby and cheerful, and from what Tom had seen so far, he seemed to be good with the junior ratings. It was worth bearing in mind, should animosity or victimization develop. Tom had a strong sense of fair play.

There were no further alarms during the remainder of the run down to the straits. In his off-watch hours Tom made it his business to talk to the hands, get to know them, find out their capabilities and try to assess their likely reliability in action. He found them a mixed bunch, but detected no lack of keenness. The HO men were, indeed, all volunteers. To date there had been no talk of conscription, but everyone knew that if the war were to last for long it was bound to come. And someone in Britain's past fighting history had said one volunteer was worth ten pressed men. Nelson?

Possibly; many things were attributed to that incredible little admiral, though in the non-naval eye he was perhaps best remembered for his liaison with Lady Hamilton . . . Three days later the *Thornton*'s slow plod brought the ship past Cape Trafalgar, and Tom thought again about Nelson and his greatest victory over the French fleet. They were all following in Nelson's footsteps now, and that was quite a thought.

They came past Europa Point and entered Gibraltar Bay as the sun declined. It was a magnificent sight as that sun went down over the small white town of Algeciras on the western edge of the bay. The bugles of the Royal Marine Light Infantry could be heard sounding for Sunset from the quarter-decks of the battleships and cruisers at the moles. It was Tom's first sight of Gibraltar and he was immensely impressed as the *Thornton* made the turn to starboard to enter the harbour between the arms of the breakwaters. The vast Rock loomed like a grey-green colossus over the warships; a military band could be heard playing at the Alameda parade-ground: the pipes and drums of a highland regiment, sounding loud and clear in the still air. There was a troopship at anchor in the bay, and Tom learned later that it was an emotional occasion, for the transport had disembarked the 1st Battalion The Argyll and Sutherland Highlanders and was standing by to embark the same regiment's 2nd Battalion on relief; and that the two battalions had not met for many years past. Brother met brother, father met son: like all the highland regiments, The Argyll and Sutherland, the 91st and 93rd Foot, was a family regiment, a clan regiment. As the *Thornton* received her berthing signal from the King's Harbour Master and proceeded across the harbour, the pipes and drums were playing 'Auld Lang Syne'. It was indeed an emotional moment . . .

As his ship came alongside her berth and the handling parties sent out the securing lines, Fletcher, standing by the engine-room telegraph, rang down Finished With Engines. For a moment he remained motionless, listening intently to the sad strains of the pipes. He caught Tom's eye.

'If that troopship is bound home, that means a relieved battalion's going to find itself in France before much longer . . .' He said no more; but Tom got his drift. 'Auld Lang Syne' was very poignant indeed. And very fitting.

The ship was put into dockyard hands next day, entering dry-dock for a bottom-scrape, for work to begin on her conversion to an HM ship and for the fitting of her armament. Apart from a shipkeeper, the whole ship's company left her for the time being, the ratings being marched to hutted accommodation in the dockyard and the officers being accommodated aboard the base depot ship, HMS *Cormorant*, an old sailing battleship, relic of days past when, as Tom had heard expressed during his own days in sail, ships were wood and men were made of iron. Now she was a travesty of what had been, her decks covered with an ungainly roof of corrugated iron. Below she was smelly and uncomfortable and infested with rats and cockroaches. Tom was allocated a small, stuffy cabin with no porthole. Fortunately at this time of year Gibraltar was not a hot place; indeed it could be very cold and wet. But on that first day Tom began to feel once again civilized. They were all back in uniform and would remain so until the ship was ready for sea and her duties as decoy. For now the flat caps, the bowler hats and the dreadful collarless shirts were thankfully gone. So was the informality insisted upon by Fletcher. There was no 'Whack' now and Petty Officer Brewster could be as pusser as he liked. Which he was.

At lunch-time that day, there was the usual gin session in *Cormorant*'s wardroom. There were guests, officers from the ships in the port, from the battleships and cruisers and torpedo-boat destroyers and submarines, officers of all branches – executive, engine-room, accountant, medical.

Much gin was drunk; there was gaiety around, some of it a little forced. Soon all the ships would be back at sea, and there was no knowing whether or not the officers would meet again. In wartime you took your pleasures as and where you found them, and the navy's pleasure was largely gin. There was laughter and after a while there was song from the younger element. There were no ladies present and they let themselves go.

> 'I don't want to join the navy
> I don't want to go to sea
> I'd rather hang around
> Piccadilly Underground
> Living on the earnings of a high-born lady . . .'

That was the most innocuous. Those that followed made no concession to the dignity of the more senior officers present; the singing progressed to the nocturnal adventures of Old King Cole, that merry old soul whose tastes in women were many and varied. After a couple of verses a four-ring captain RN put a stop to it.

Tom left the wardroom with the *Thornton*'s medical officer, Grant-Wylie. They walked into the town, coming into Waterport Street near the Bristol Hotel, which seemed to Tom to act as a kind of overflow of the wardrooms of the fleet, naval officers coming and going. Gibraltar was all navy and army, the locals swamped by the exigencies of the war. Gibraltar stood sentinel over the approaches to the Mediterranean.

'The Rock'll maybe act as a convincing barrier to the U-boats,' Tom said, following out his own thoughts. 'The strait's narrow enough as it is.'

'Well, they can't be detected submerged, don't forget. And if they get through, then that's where we come in.'

Tom nodded. 'Us and others. There should be plenty of

action to keep us busy.' He paused, glancing sideways at the doctor. 'How d'you feel about it?'

'Well, I suppose I joined for action. I'm just not too sure I've enough experience to cope, that's all. I did my clerking, of course, in surgery . . . patched up a few limbs, did an appendectomy or two with a registrar standing by. Now I'm on my own, at least when we're at sea. And of course I've no practical experience of gunshot wounds, the results of shells and so on.'

'I don't suppose many other surgeons have, old man. It's a longish time since the South African war. Anyway – no point in worrying.'

Grant-Wylie's face was creased with his anxieties. He was by nature a worrier. After volunteering for the RNVR he'd done a course in war surgery at the Royal Naval Hospital at Stonehouse in Plymouth, but the course had been short and theoretical and he didn't believe he'd taken it all in as he should have done. There were reasons for this, or one reason anyway – and that was a girl. He had got her pregnant, a bad mark for a doctor, and it was worrying him a lot. Sometimes, guiltily, he wondered about his motives for volunteering for the navy. It could be a way of avoiding his responsibilities. Or at least of distancing himself from them.

He said nothing of those worries to Tom. They walked along Waterport Street, right to the end where British territory ended at the neutral ground, the wasteland between the frontier posts of Britain and Spain. Distantly could be seen the shiny black headgear of the *Guardia Civile*, and their green uniforms as they lounged outside their guardroom. Spain, a land at peace but one with ever half an eye cast on the reclaiming of the Rock that had once been theirs.

Tom and the doctor turned about and walked back the way they had come. Grant-Wylie went back aboard the depot ship. He would spend some time studying his medical and surgical textbooks. Tom went ahead, past the Governor's residence with sentries of The Argyll and Sutherland Highlanders giving him a smart butt salute as he walked by. He passed the picquet house that formed the guardroom of the Naval Provost Marshal, under the arch of the South Port, and down into the dockyard by way of the Ragged Staff Gate. He went on towards the dry-dock where the *Thornton* was lying on the chocks. Really, he didn't know why he'd come; he'd be seeing plenty of the ship later on. But for some reason or other he'd developed a feeling for the old collier. She was a veteran of the seas, a willing workhorse, unglamorous but sturdy. Unpretentious. And she was going to have a very dangerous job to do, luring the U-boats to the surface, risking her old plates against the torpedoes and gunfire of a very determined enemy.

She looked forlorn and neglected in the dry-dock, helpless out of her natural element. The Spanish dockyard workers had not yet started on her much-barnacled bottom. Tom knew from his days on the South American run that the spirit of *mañana* ran very deep in Spanish hearts.

It was a depressing sight. Tom turned away and went back to the *Cormorant.*

SEVEN

NEXT MORNING, AFTER ATTENDING A conference in the Tower, the headquarters of Rear-Admiral Gibraltar, Lieutenant-Commander Fletcher went down to the dry-dock with his officers. 'I like to keep an eye on things,' he said. 'If the dockyard authorities see me as an interfering bastard, then so be it.' He paused. 'I have news, Number One,' he went on to Stallybrass. 'We're no longer to be known as the s.s. *Thornton*. When we're ready for sea we're to be commissioned into naval service as His Majesty's Ship *Geelong*.'

'Why an Australian name?' Stallybrass asked.

Fletcher shrugged. 'Don't ask me. As a matter of fact most of the Q ships have been given Australian names. *Werribee*, *Wonganella*, *Baralong* for instance. My guess would be that with all the new construction coming along, the Admiralty naming committee's running out of ideas.'

Stallybrass nodded. Tom asked, 'Still cloth caps, sir?'

'I'm afraid so, yes, once we're operational. There's still the security aspect – in fact we'll still have *Thornton* painted on the stern with Cardiff as our port of registration.'

'But if we're going to be HMS *Geelong*, surely –'

Fletcher laughed and laid a hand on Tom's shoulder. 'You need patience and a strong sense of the ridiculous to learn all the ways of the King's service, Chatto. We'll be *Geelong* on paper only – in the Admiralty's files and in the Navy List. Everything has to be . . . well, *regularized* is perhaps the word. Another word is bullshit. But we'll actually be in every sense an HM ship in spite of what I've just been saying. Does that make any kind of sense?'

Tom kept a straight face. 'No, sir. None at all. But I suppose we just accept it as being something to do with that security angle.'

'That's the kindest way of looking at it. Admirals have to earn their keep by thinking up ideas to baffle those of us who go to sea. But we'll not lose any sleep over it. Now – once the work's started on the ship, I'd like one of my executive officers to be on hand during the dockyard working hours. Number One, I'd like you to work out an Officer of the Day rota. What about you, Chief?' he added to Mr Wenstock.

'They'll not be messing about with my engines, sir,' Wenstock said. 'Not beyond a few small repair items that the dockyard can see to. Nothing urgent. But while the Spaniards are on the ship I'll see to it that either me or my chief ERA is around. I'm not having things mucked around with that shouldn't be mucked around with.'

Coming from the hutted accommodation allocated to the lower deck, Petty Officer Brewster was making similar resolutions. He was having no dagoes messing about with his deck gear. Left to themselves they'd very likely take a siesta in the lifeboat, for instance, even crap on the deck if they felt like it, too bloody tired to use the shoreside heads provided for them. No, he was having none of that, thank you very much. Brewster was feeling peeved. Never mind the security, which was often enough a joke at the best of times, the master-at-arms at *Cormorant* had already passed on the buzz that the *Thornton* was to be renamed but had added what was in fact the obvious, that the cloth-cap image would persist at sea. Brewster had known this but hadn't been able to stop himself hoping for a miracle once the ship was well and truly in the Med. Wearing once again his PO's uniform with crossed gold anchors on his left upper arm, his white-topped cap with gold and red badge with another anchor, the sort of cap that made saluting a pleasure, he felt back to normal. It would be terrible to go back to Whack; yet he comforted himself with the certainty that 'Whack' was only for propaganda purposes when there were potential spies around, like the dock loafers back in Barry. Out at sea, whatever the garments, the skipper was going to be pusser. And when they came to grips with the Jerries, the rotten buggers would know the cloth caps and collarless shirts were certainly not the real thing. Bloody Jerries! Petty Officer Brewster couldn't wait for the gunport doors to go down and flaunt the Union flag . . . what those daft ha'porths who didn't know called the Union Jack. Nothing was a jack unless it was worn at the jackstaff, any fool ought to know that . . .

The work began; the *Geelong* ex *Thornton* didn't spend all that long in the dry-dock. The bottom-scrape and subsequent red-lead paint left her with what Leading Seaman Tubbs called a lovely shiny new arse. That and a few other jobs done, the dock was flooded and the old ship rose from the chocks and was hauled out by the tugs to be berthed at the south mole ahead of the battleship *Collingwood*, one of the St Vincent class carrying ten 12-inch guns as her main armament. Leading Seaman Tubbs had an old mate aboard the *Collingwood*, a Yeoman of Signals that he'd been shipmates with when the yeoman had been a leading hand. They met in a bar in Waterport Street where Brickwood's beer was available to remind them of Pompey. They compared notes, talked of the old days when King Edward had been on the throne, and booze and tarts had been the lifeblood of Malta when the Mediterranean fleet was blocking up the Grand Harbour. They talked of Strada Stretta, where every other establishment was a bar, and the rest were knocking shops, all well patronized.

They talked also of personalities past and present. And past and present mingled when Leading Seaman Tubbs mentioned Petty Officer Brewster.

The yeoman from the *Collingwood* gave a whistle of

sympathy. 'Shit a brick,' he said. Which summed up Petty Officer Brewster.

Tubbs was much in evidence when the fitting of the guns began. That was his province, along with Mr Chatto. Tom's good opinion of his right-hand man was confirmed; Tubbs was a hard and conscientious worker. There was a good deal to be done: parts of the ship had to be strengthened to take the 4.7-inch main armament. This involved a lot of cutting with torches, and the use of rivets, as did the cutting of the ship's side plating to make the hinged sections for the gunports on either side. There was work to be done on the bridge for the fitting of the machine-guns in the port and starboard wings. Once the gun-fitting began, Fletcher was almost continually aboard with Tom and the First Lieutenant. Tom was involved both as gunnery officer and as navigator. In the latter capacity he would need to be present when the dockyard's compass adjuster came aboard to swing the ship for deviation and some knowledge as to where new metal had been inserted would be an advantage.

The job was not going to be finished on time, and after the work was completed the ship would need to be cleaned throughout. Fletcher exploded when the dockyard foreman gave him the new completion date. He blasted off to Stallybrass. 'I suppose it's to be expected of the Spanish. More accustomed to refitting donkeys.'

'I've known worse,' Stallybrass said with a grin.

'For God's sake, man . . . where?'

'Ireland, sir. Cork. We had to put in for repairs when I was in Canadian Pacific, an engine breakdown slap off the port. All promises and no do. "Ah, sure, you'll be all set in the morning." And that was the last we heard for a week.'

'Well,' Fletcher said, 'I'm going to find a stick of dynamite. Its name is the Chief of Staff at the Tower.' And off he went, seething. He was anxious to get to sea; they all were. As yet they hadn't got a fully worked-up ship's company.

*

All in all, they were in Gibraltar for seven weeks. Seven weeks of little in the way of exercise on the Rock apart from football matches arranged against teams from other warships. Plenty of bar time was put in; a lot of that Brickwood's beer was consumed by the ratings and a good deal of gin by the officers in *Cormorant's* wardroom as well. Fletcher kept an eye on that; without wishing to be a wet blanket, he was going to need clear heads when at last they went to sea. And all the time the war news kept coming in as reported by the *Gibraltar Chronicle.* Things were not going well on the Western Front. Sir John French, the British Commander-in-Chief, along with General Joffre of France, was expected shortly to mount the big push that for some while had been on everyone's lips; but as yet a date had not materialized. At sea the news was bad too. One after another, the merchant ships, lifeblood of the country, were going down to the U-boats and the commerce raiders. Too many of the sinkings were taking place in the Mediterranean. The services of the *Geelong* were much needed. More sticks of dynamite were employed by the naval staff in the Tower.

At last after the perennially filthy business of coaling ship, they were ready for the compass adjuster. Once he had done his job he would be transferred to a dockyard launch and the ship would go at once to sea.

The day before that scheduled for leaving port, there had been other news – news of a personal sort for Tom Chatto, conveyed in a cable from Ireland. The Dean of Moyna had regretfully been given his marching orders by his Bishop. And what Tom had feared had come about. His sister-in-law Edith had overcome her headaches for long enough to offer the old man temporary sanctuary in Edward's rectory but was fixing up a lodging in Galway City. Brother Philip had not been able to help; he was back in France waiting for Sir John French to move. Edith thought Tom ought to know.

Tom read between the lines: Edith thought he ought to know what a noble martyr she was being.

So this was the end. The end of his boyhood's home, all he had known, a final break with the memory of his mother. And what a sad old man his father was going to be, bereft of his garden, left to potter with nothing to do from one long day to another. And the population of Galway was overwhelmingly Roman Catholic. The chances of finding a Protestant landlady would be minimal. The Dean would feel abandoned to the idolaters. But possibly this wouldn't happen. Edith was rabidly anti-Roman. She might not be willing to deliver even her father-in-law to the Pope.

But all in all it was not the best news to get just before sailing to war.

The *Geelong* headed outwards into Gibraltar Bay and turned eastward past Europa Point to head into the Mediterranean where she would start her patrol. Tom was on the bridge with Fletcher as they took their departure from Europa. The ship felt different after her conversion; it was heartening to have the proximity of the armament below and in the bridge wings. The bulwarks, the bridge screens, were now backed up by the lashed hammocks of the ratings; as a collier, the ship had been fitted with bunks in the seamen's accommodation below the fo'c'sle, and there had been cabins for the petty officers – the bosun and the carpenter, also the cook, steward and engine-room donkeyman; these now being occupied by Brewster, Popplewell and the engine-room artificers and stoker POs. The hammocks formed extra protection for the bridge and wheelhouse against enemy machine-gun fire.

Once at sea the working-up of the ship's company began, the moulding of all hands into one efficient fighting unit. Gun drill was held constantly under the immediate orders of Leading Seaman Tubbs and overseen by Tom. Speed of reaction was of the first importance. Again and again Tom timed the manoeuvre from the moment of an imaginary sighting of a conning-tower breaking surface to the moment when the gunport door went down, the 4.7 was revealed, the White Ensign was hoisted to the ensign staff and the first shell was ready to be sent off. Using a stopwatch, he kept the guns' crews hard at it. The timing had to be reduced to the absolute minimum and until that possible minimum was established and kept to, or perhaps exceeded, in the succeeding drills there would be no respite.

Petty Officer Brewster was concerned with things other than gunnery. As chief boatswain's mate he was responsible, under the First Lieutenant, for the efficient working of the deck gear: the anchors and cables, ropes and wires, the falls for lowering the lifeboat if such was required, as Brewster knew it would be for the 'panic party'. And maybe to save their own lives too.

Fletcher had spoken to all hands back in Gibraltar, before the compass adjuster had come aboard, of the 'panic party'.

'It's a vital part of our job,' he'd said. 'Remember, we have to appear to the submarine's crew to be just a tramp ship with no experience of war and gunfire. The first reaction of a tramp ship without protection would be to abandon before being sunk by gunfire . . . in the hope that they'd be picked up and taken aboard.' He paused. 'I'm not suggesting that tramp crews are given to panicking – they're not, and the term's a slander on them. But it's been dreamed up by the Admiralty as a useful way of describing it. We have to appear to panic by lowering a boat and pulling away fast. Basically, that's all there is to it. The First Lieutenant will be detailing a "panic party" as soon as we're away.'

As the hands dismissed about their part-of-ship duties under Petty Officer Brewster, Fletcher had a separate word with Tom. 'Sailors love arsing about when they have official sanction. I'm going to put it to Brewster, get him to give 'em a free hand in making a convincing balls-up of lowering the boat when the time comes. Show real panic. They'll love it . . . especially the humorists among them.'

Not so Petty Officer Brewster. Brewster was no humorist himself. He had been somewhat shocked by what was in effect an order. He never made a balls-up of anything; Yorkshiremen simply didn't and that was all there was to it. And as for *conniving* at slovenliness . . . well! He vibrated beneath his resumed cloth cap. 'Never heard the like I haven't,' he said gratingly to Petty Officer Popplewell, feeling able to blow off steam about the officers to someone who was his equal (not *quite* equal; Popplewell was With But After, so to speak, but never mind). 'Whatever next, eh? Buggered if I'm going to encourage matloes what's cack-handed enough already . . . encourage 'em to make a charlie of me is what it comes to, eh?'

Petty Officer Popplewell scratched his head and said mildly, 'Bit o' yumour doesn't come amiss. Lighter side o' war you might say.'

'Bollocks. *You* might, I don't.'

Brewster marched away, swinging his arms as usual, mouth set in a thin line of fury. Why in God's name had he not been given a draft chit for something like the *Temeraire* or the brand-new battle-cruiser *Tiger* where there was a four-ring skipper and an admiral plus a commander who would come down like a ton of bricks on a seaboat arse-ended in the hoggin such as *this* skipper seemed to be suggesting? Making his way along the after well-deck past the hatch of the empty hold as the *Geelong* nosed into the swiftly falling dark of the Mediterranean night, with a myriad stars hanging so low in the clear sky that they seemed almost within arm's reach, he heard a voice coming, as he believed, from the after accommodation below the poop, a place where the engine-room ratings – the black gang Brewster called them – lived.

The voice was singing; softly, but loud enough for Brewster to hear.

'Fick-fack, Paddywhack, give the dog a bone . . .'

Brewster stood for a moment stock-still, his face suffused with angry blood, fists clenched at his sides. Then he did an about-turn and marched into the alleyway below the poop. No one there. He made a hissing sound then shouted into the silence. 'If I catch anyone offering me bloody cheek like that, I'll fuckin' *throttle* him so I will!'

Fletcher had heard Brewster's shout. It had been virtually a screech. He left the bridge and called down to the PO from the deck outside his cabin. 'Petty Officer Brewster.'

Brewster halted. 'Sir?'

'You seemed to have some sort of trouble, Brewster.'

'Yessir. Impertinence, sir, from them buggers aft. Beg pardon, sir. The stokers.' Brewster stiffened a sudden resolve. You didn't cheek officers, you certainly didn't reprimand the skipper – God forbid – but this was perhaps the best opportunity he'd ever get. So he chanced his arm. 'Beg pardon, sir,' he said again. 'If I might make a request, sir. A personal request like, sir.'

'By all means.'

'It's to do with "Whack", sir. What you addressed me as back in Barry Dock, sir.' Brewster coughed in some embarrassment. 'If you was perhaps to like *vary* it, sir. That's to say like, call me summat else, sir. With respect, sir, I'd be obliged.'

Fletcher said gravely, 'I'm always glad to oblige my senior ratings, Brewster. I take it you refer to those occasions when it behoves us not to appear too RN?'

'Yessir, that's it, sir. If –'

'What would you like me to call you under those circumstances, Brewster?'

'Well, sir.' Brewster thought; he did see the skipper's problem. Up to a point. He asked, 'What about PO, sir? Just plain PO?'

Fletcher's tongue was in his cheek when he said, 'I've a better idea. What about Mister?'

'Yessir!' Brewster was delighted. 'I reckon that's the thing. Thank you, sir.'

Fletcher went back to the bridge. It was Tom's watch. Fletcher reported the conversation, keeping his voice down. 'I felt inclined to agree to PO. Not Pee Oh, that is. Po, as in bedroom utensil. If it hadn't been bad for discipline I would have, but Brewster wouldn't have seen the funny side. I'd like to shoot the so-and-so that sent me Brewster as buffer . . .'

There were those on the lower deck who were developing a similar desire. One of these was a grizzled able seaman, a three-badgeman (or had been), an RFR man just pushing fifty which was a good deal older than bloody Brewster. Able Seaman Higgins was a first-rate hand and knew it – a sailor of the old school, very dependable. He was also a grandfather, which in his view gave him a sort of status that shouldn't have allowed him to be pushed around by a whipper-snapper of a jumped-up petty officer not long out of the cradle. Able Seaman Higgins knew that was an exaggeration, but still; that was the way he felt. And before they'd left Gib, the bugger had run him in to the Officer of the Day on the accommodation huts for bottling his tot, the daily rum issue which all hands below the rate of petty officer were supposed to drink on the spot. Supposed to. At Higgins' age he reckoned that was a load of tommy-rot, bottling his tot being something he felt entitled to do. There was always birthdays coming up somewhere that needed celebrating . . . anyway, Brewster had snooped and found the flask and that was that. Up before Jimmy the One, then the skipper, and his good conduct badges gone for a burton. He didn't hold it against the skipper; the navy's discipline was harsh and the skipper had had no choice. Higgins admitted cheeking Brewster and disobeying the order to stand up when spoken to by a petty officer, a fairly heinous crime in itself. But those badges: their loss meant a reduction in Higgins' daily rate of pay and also, when the war ended and he was once again on the beach, his pension would be affected likewise. All bloody Brewster's doing. Sod it, ratings had been bottling their tots and petty officers had been turning blind eyes to it ever since Nelson's day, more or less. Likely even Nelson did it when no one was looking, or would've if officers had drawn tots.

Able Seaman Higgins seethed thereafter each time he came into contact with Brewster. But let the bugger wait. Over the long years of British sea supremacy unpopular, bullying, toadying petty officers had now and again disappeared from sight at sea. Wait for a spell of filthy weather and high seas that swept the decks, get the bugger in a corner, bash his head in with a blunt instrument and chuck him overboard, maybe lashed down into a wash-deck locker that just happened to have come adrift. Very final and all questions parried when the PO's absence became known, by which time the bugger would be many miles astern. Bland innocence: 'Didn't see a thing, sir.' 'Me eyes was on lookout, sir.' 'Never 'eard nothing, sir.' 'Disliked, sir? Oh no, sir, not disliked, sir. Very pusser 'e was, what he should be, but 'e was always fair, sir. Bad luck on 'is missus, sir.'

No witnesses. Oh yes, it could be done.

It wasn't exactly a patrol; it was the trailing of a net, a fishing expedition to catch a U-boat. The *Geelong* proceeded easterly, ostensibly with a cargo of coal for Taranto in the heel of Italy's boot. For most of the time there was a cold wind blowing, an easterly wind from the Holy Land into which the ship butted, plunging and rolling with a sick-making motion. Many of the hands were suffering still, as was Dr Grant-Wylie, whose unruly stomach was adding to his private worries about the girl he'd left behind. Whilst in Gibraltar mail had come out from home. The baby would be born within the next two months, and Grant-Wylie knew the extreme unlikelihood of his being back in the UK before then. The girl was worried sick; she'd been given a hard time by her parents for whom the whole thing was the most terrible disgrace, they being of the shotgun-wedding persuasion, an outlook in which they were of course not alone. Grant-Wylie very nearly prayed for a miracle, a miracle involving the *Geelong* being sunk by a U-boat without any loss of life, an occurrence that would send him home on survivors' leave. Unless they were captured by the Germans . . . not a very useful prayer.

Another to receive news had been Mr Wenstock. Wenstock's wife had been admitted once again to hospital in Pompey. His daughter wrote to say that the doctors suspected stomach cancer. Wenstock had kept the news to himself; cancer was a word you didn't ever mention and he was surprised that his daughter should have written it. Euphemisms were always better. They left room for hope.

There had been more news for Tom Chatto: a letter, this time with good news. The rector of St James's Collegiate Church in Galway, a widower with a housekeeper, a cook and a parlourmaid, had taken pity on an old colleague and had offered him accommodation and companionship. Tom, again reading between the lines, had sensed Edith's immense relief. A letter had also come from Grace Handley. This had arrived the day the *Geelong* had left Gibraltar, and Tom was thinking about it during an afternoon watch when a report came down from the masthead lookout in the crow's nest.

EIGHT

'BEARING GREEN ONE-OH, SIR! LOOKS like a periscope, sir!'

Tom steadied his binoculars on the bearing. The surface was disturbed and a periscope was not easy to pick up in the kerfuffle. But . . . yes, there was something. No chances were to be taken.

Tom ran for the voice-pipe and wrenched back the brass cover. 'Captain, sir . . . periscope sighted off the starboard bow . . . distance four cables, sir.'

'Right! Panic party to muster, close up guns' crews, stand by to open gunport doors. Warn the engine-room. I'll be up directly.'

Fletcher was on the bridge within fifteen seconds and looking towards the bearing through his binoculars. 'It's a periscope right enough.' He looked round as Petty Officer Brewster came to the bridge. 'Ah – Brewster. We have the enemy. We do absolutely nothing until he surfaces – that's important – nothing overt that is. But be ready to lower away the seaboat for the panic party.'

'Aye, aye, sir.' Brewster saluted, went red with chagrin when he realized that in his current role of Mister he didn't salute, turned away and slid fast down the ladder to the deck. He spotted Able Seaman Higgins and opened his mouth for a loud shout when he realized that that, too, would be out of order. They were not supposed to have seen the periscope, but the periscope had seen them so they must show no reaction. Brewster's voice became a low hiss. 'Move your arse, Higgins, and muster the lowerers of the watch. They're to stand by the falls but out o' sight, all right?'

On the bridge Fletcher said, 'I'll take over up here, Chatto. You'd better stand by the 4.7, starboard side.' He turned to the leading signalman, acting Yeoman of Signals. 'Yeoman, have the battle ensign ready to hoist.'

'Bent on now, sir.'

'Good man.' Fletcher pushed the bowler hat farther back on his forehead. He was still watching the bearing closely but not appearing to, and was not using binoculars now. The periscope was still there but had drawn a little aft. The moment was an apprehensive one. The U-boat was so far giving no hint of being about to surface. If she remained submerged, then it could be expected that she would fire a torpedo. She had the *Geelong* fair and square in her sights; she could hardly miss. And the one torpedo would be all she needed. Chatto and the starboard 4.7 crew would go up in fragments of flesh; the U-boat's point of aim would for a certainty be amidships. Then the *Geelong* would go down, her back broken, her decks aflame until she settled in the water by which time the ammunition stowed in the magazine would very likely have blown up as well.

There was nothing Fletcher could do other than remain a sitting duck until the German showed his hand a little more.

He moved to the engine-room voice-pipe, still watching the bearing. 'Chief – Captain here. It's still touch and go. I'm going to need a good head of steam for manoeuvring if she surfaces. But have an eye, Chief, to a bloody fast evacuation from below.'

'You mean if she opens, sir.'

Wenstock's voice was flat, no emotion. He knew the score; the men in the engine-room were goners the moment a torpedo hit. No chance of escape, no chance at all of making it up the spider's-web of slippery steel ladders to the open deck. Potentially, they were already in their coffins, screwed down tight and all. Fletcher knew this as well as Wenstock did. He said evenly, 'Abandon without further orders if we're hit.' That, too, was bull – and they both knew that as well, but you had to say something, had to be optimistic. Down there on the starting-platform, Mr Wenstock, warrant engineer of much experience and husband of a very sick wife, prayed with closed eyes that the bloody Hun wouldn't find the old tramp worth one of his valuable tin fish.

Minutes passed. It seemed like hours. Amidships at the gunport door, they waited in a tense silence for orders from the bridge. Hands stood ready to send the gunport door crashing down to reveal the Union flag and the deadly snout of the 4.7 protruding from the gunshield. It all had to be done very fast, very fast indeed. Tom stood by the voice-pipe from the bridge, ready for the off, the word for battle. A tic started up at the side of Leading Seaman Tubbs' mouth. At the breech end of the gun Petty Officer Brewster had stood a minute earlier, checking up before going on deck to supervise the panic party. Brewster, Tubbs thought, would likely start a panic of his own when he started bawling the odds. Brewster's thoughts, one-track-minded as he was, revolved around his cloth cap and the rest of his clothing. Say the Jerry captured them. What a way to go to a POW camp for the duration! They might well not believe him when he said he was a petty officer. Not without his cap they wouldn't; and he didn't fancy spending the rest of the war as a sort of mobile scran-bag.

Now the periscope was obvious. It had risen a little more and the feather of streaming water could be seen clearly. To ignore it might be suspicious: no ship's lookout could have missed it. And now the maximum time had to be gained, time before the U-boat surfaced if she was going to, time before her crew could emerge from below and man their fo'c'sle-mounted gun. In Fletcher's view she would surface; she was too close now for her own safety to use a torpedo and would opt for gunfire; but he might as well make certain, assure the U-boat Captain that he had no need to waste the Kaiser's money.

He leaned over the after guardrail and called down to the deck. 'Lower away, panic party . . . and act for all you're worth. Petty Officer Brewster?'

'Yessir?'

'Look scared.'

Bloody hell. How did you do that? Suddenly Brewster found out for himself: he *was* scared. He'd never faced shot and shell before, in fact none of them had. It was as yet early in the war, and until the engagement off Coronel a few months earlier there hadn't been a naval action for donkey's years except for the Taku Forts in China. So he didn't need to act much. He yapped at the lowerers to cast off the gripes of the seaboat and start the falls, yapped at the panic party to embark with orders to pull in any direction so long as it was away from the ship, supposedly doomed. Most of the lowerers, most of the panic party, were HO men and cack-handed ones at that, despite recent drills. They had no need to act. The for'ard fall went down faster than the after one and the boat upended. Some of the hands clung fast to the fall, thus stopping it going out any farther; others fell into the sea. There was shouting and yelling and the lowerers fell over each other on deck. Brewster blasphemed, but knew that this was precisely what the skipper wanted. Those who'd fallen in the drink would have to wait.

An authorized balls-up; and it had played its part. At the height of the shambles, the German Captain evidently saw his chance. A squat black shape emerged from the water, tilted as the bows rose with water streaming back over the pressure hull to the base of the conning-tower.

Fletcher opened the voice-pipe to the starboard gunport.

'Open gunport door, Chatto, and stand by.' Then he spoke to the Yeoman of Signals. 'Hoist battle ensign!'

The White Ensign was hoisted to the mainmasthead. Fletcher used the voice-pipe to the guns once more.

'Fire when ready.'

'Ready, sir.' Tom gave the order. '*Open fire!*'

With the gunport door down to reveal the Union flag to the enemy, the 4.7 crashed out; there was a blast of flame, a cloud of acrid gunsmoke. The recoil came back, the crew standing clear as drilled into them by Leading Seaman Tubbs and Tom himself. The first shell fell short of the target; the second was over. By now the German had reacted. Machine-gun fire swept the *Geelong*'s decks and there was a crash as the U-boat's fo'c'sle gun opened. A shell took the water some distance to port. Another, a good example of the efficiency of the German naval gunners, took the mainmast and brought down the White Ensign amid a crash and tangle of woodwork, wire and rope. Another took the fo'c'sle-head, smashing both port and starboard anchor cables and their slips, and causing damage to the hawse-pipes. But Leading Seaman Tubbs was a very good gunlayer: his third shot took the base of the conning-tower; his next took out the fo'c'sle gun-mounting, mangling its crew and leaving the vessel virtually defenceless. From the bridge, Fletcher saw that the damage to the conning-tower was probably such that the U-boat would be unable to submerge.

He took up his megaphone and shouted across the water. 'I suggest you surrender, Captain. If you guarantee no more machine-gun fire, I'll take off you and your crew. Otherwise you'll be sunk by gunfire.'

There seemed to be a conference in the conning-tower. There was no more firing. After some five minutes of apparent argument, the U-boat Captain was seen to wave a fist in the air. 'Perfidious British pigs! Yes, I surrender.'

Petty Officer Brewster sorted out the tangle of the seaboat's falls and this time the boat's crew were a model of seamanship – more or less – as they pulled across to the now motionless submarine, picking up the men who had gone overboard on the way. The boat made several journeys to bring off the Germans; some of them swam across and were helped aboard the *Geelong* by the use of lines and scrambling nets. They were met by an armed guard under Petty Officer Popplewell, and were mustered in the fore well-deck under the eye of the bridge. In the meantime the damage reports reached Fletcher. And the casualty reports: none dead but four with various injuries, burns, broken limbs, bullet wounds – work for the surgeon probationer. Before speaking to his prisoners, Fletcher conferred with Stallybrass and Tom. 'The German isn't submergworthy, but she's probably seaworthy. I'll have a check round shortly. If she's fit for sea, I'll take her in tow and head for Malta.'

The word went round the ship in no time at all. There could be prize money. The ship's company were unsure of the legal position but there was room for hope. Anyway, Malta would be worth a run ashore. And they'd enter the Grand Harbour with the visible evidence of their achievement. That would entitle them to a swagger when the *dghaisas* landed the libertymen at Custom House Steps. Already they all felt a lot better for the action; but they knew it could be a different story next time.

The U-boat's crew was taken under the armed guard to the fore hold, entering by way of the tween-deck. There were no sleeping arrangements and they would be highly uncomfortable, the more so if the wind increased. But the *Geelong* was not so far off Malta: the ETA as worked out by Tom was some seventy-two hours ahead. The German officers were spared the hold; they were given the use of two double-berthed cabins in the engineers' accommodation aft below the poop, and an armed sentry was placed on the doors. Before they were led away Fletcher had words with the U-boat captain, one *Kapitän-leutnant* Heinrich Keichle. The German was informed of Fletcher's intention to take the U-boat in tow.

Fletcher asked, 'In your view, Captain, is she seaworthy?'

The German shrugged, his eyes cold and fish-like. 'For yourself you must find out.'

'That I shall do, don't worry.'

Fletcher said no more. There would be no further questions; he had to bear in mind that a captured enemy was not obliged to part with any information that could be useful to the other side. Any discreet probing was better left to the naval or military intelligence officers in the Malta command.

Stallybrass, the RNR First Lieutenant, was sent across with the *Geelong*'s shipwright and an engine-room artificer to carry out a survey. 'Fast as possible, Number One,' Fletcher said. There was danger in lying stopped; other U-boats could be in the vicinity. So the check round was carried out swiftly. When the survey party returned aboard, Stallybrass reported the submarine watertight throughout the hull, the only leakage being from the base of the conning-tower and from the mounting of the shattered fo'c'sle gun.

'Easily enough contained by the pumps, sir,' Stallybrass reported. 'So long as we don't get heavy weather, anyway.'

Fletcher nodded. 'And the conning-tower itself?'

'Damaged, and the hatch can't be shut – again, that could be tricky in a blow, sir.'

'We'll risk it.' Fletcher made up his mind. 'Nothing like a capture, Number One.' All the ship's executive officers were with Fletcher on the bridge. He asked, 'Which of you has previous experience of handling a ship under tow, gentlemen?'

There was a pause. Tom's mind went back to the *Orvega* and the semi-derelict windjammer *Falls of Dochart* that they had encountered in appalling weather not far off Cape Horn; he thought of the desperate efforts to board the ship and then pass a tow in an attempt to salvage the stricken ship with the few hands left alive after the *Falls of Dochart* had been dismasted . . . He said, 'I have, sir. A ship under sail.'

'Rather a different kettle of fish . . . in fact a tougher one than what we have now, I'd imagine. How d'you feel about temporary command of a submarine, Chatto?'

'If you think I can manage it, sir.'

'It's not what *I* think, it's what *you* think. Can you cope?'

Tom said, 'Yes, I can.'

'Good! Then the job's yours. Find out which, if any, of the hands have towing experience and choose who you want. I'd suggest a PO plus a leading hand and four. And someone from the engine-room. Also I'll have a word with the German lower-deck men. It would be handy to have someone with you who knows the boat, and the hands may not be quite so sticky as their Captain. Now.' He looked Tom directly in the eyes. 'Your PO. Do me a favour – take Brewster. Whatever else he may be, he's a good seaman. But I regret to say he riles me.'

Fletcher was a persuasive man. He found a degree of co-operation in the *Geelong*'s fore hold. He had held out a carrot: no promises, but assistance rendered might find a favourable reaction in Malta and in the POW camp in Britain when the prisoners were transported. The man who volunteered despite hostile mutterings from some of his shipmates proved useful: an engine-room artificer named Ernst Kleberbaum, who was a good English-speaker. With the German rating Tom's party was made up of Petty Officer Brewster, a leading seaman named Harkness, plus Able Seaman Barrett, three other junior seaman ratings and an ERA, and one of the RNVR lieutenants, Frank Newman. While Stallybrass and Petty Officer Popplewell made ready on the poop for towing aft, Tom went away in the seaboat with his party to make ready the U-boat's gear for being taken in tow. In case of need both officers were armed with revolvers.

On arrival aboard Tom went with Brewster along the plating of the pressure hull, past the remains of the gun-mounting, to the bullring in the bows. On either side of the bows there were ring-bolts set into the hull. Tom examined them.

'What do you think?' he asked Brewster.

'To take the towing pendant, sir, do you mean? Yes, I'd say they were put there for that very purpose like.'

Tom nodded. 'D'you know anything about submarines, Petty Officer Brewster?'

Brewster answered promptly and scornfully. 'Not a bleedin' thing, sir. Dirty way o' fighting if you asks me, sir. Me, I done my time with the proper fleet, the dreadnoughts like, and what I says is –'

'Yes, all right, Brewster, I quite understand. Right – we'll use the ring-bolts.' He used his knowledge of semaphore to inform the *Geelong* that he was ready to take the tow. Word came back that the towing pendant was ready at the bitts aft. As they watched from the U-boat's plating the *Geelong* moved to position herself a cable's-length ahead. The eye of the towing pendant was seen leading from the bitts and fairlead to hang over the stern and when Tom gave a wave it was paid out to be taken in hand by the seaboat's crew who brought it across to the U-boat's bows, a grass line with a steel-wire hawser about half-way along its length, the wire's weight intended to keep the tow safely beneath the water.

There was something of a struggle as the hands tried to take the eye of the towing pendant through the bullring and then lead it through the port-side ring-bolt, then across the deck to the starboard one where it would be secured. There were some bruised fingers, a good deal of swearing and some bad temper from Petty Officer Brewster who seemed set on doing things his own way, a way that seemed to Tom Chatto to indicate that Brewster didn't really know what he was doing despite Fletcher's reference to the PO's good seamanship.

Tom did what he hadn't wanted to do: he overrode Brewster, motioning him away from the hands for the sake of privacy.

'Through the ring-bolt this way, Petty Officer Brewster.'

'Oh no, sir. With respect, sir. Not for me to disagree with an officer, o' course, sir.' There was more than a touch of sarcasm, which Tom chose to ignore. 'What I'd do, sir –'

'I'm sorry, Petty Officer Brewster –'

'So am I, sir, very sorry. But the way I'm handling that towing pendant, sir, is what I seen done time and again in the fleet, under the eyes, sir, the very eyes of Admiral Lord Fisher and – and the like. On exercises, like – manoeuvres.'

'I see. Where was this?'

'Where was it, sir? In the Channel, sir –'

'In fair weather?'

'O' course in fair weather, sir. Off Portland . . . you don't exercise towing stations, sir, in anything *but* fair weather, could be dangerous could that. Too risky like.' Brewster shook his head dourly.

'I have done it myself,' Tom said mildly.

'Oh, yes, sir? And where *was* that, sir, might I ask?'

'Off Cape Horn. In a full easterly gale with the ship dismasted.'

Brewster's mouth closed with a snap and he went very red. He kept his trap shut thereafter.

The tow was passed in safety. Tom signalled back that he was ready to proceed. Thirty seconds later the water was seen to froth up below the *Geelong*'s counter and, very gently at first, the slack of the towing pendant was taken up, the rope with its wire spring lifting from the sea, dripping water and coming for a while bar-taut. As the U-boat began to move ahead the tow slackened a little, dipping beneath the water which was how it should remain.

When the U-boat was moving easily and the right amount of strain had settled on the tow, Tom led the hands back along the casing to the conning-tower, a guard being maintained on the German. They went down through the hatch into the close stuffiness of the interior, Newman, the RNVR lieutenant, remaining to take the first watch in the conning-tower while Tom made a quick inspection of the U-boat below decks.

NINE

PETTY OFFICER BREWSTER ACCOMPANIED Tom. He sniffed the air. 'Stinks, sir,' he said. 'Boat's filthy. Bah goom, I never thought the Jerries'd be living like pigs. Not that they isn't pigs,' he added, 'way they carry on like.'

The submarine was indeed filthy. There was a smell of food gone sour that in places overlaid the smells of oil and the lingering acrid fumes of cordite that had gone down the hatch when the conning-tower had been hit. The tiny galley overflowed with unwashed dishes. Articles of clothing lay around the confined space that acted as the ratings' mess-deck, and in the curtained-off recess that formed the officers' accommodation. The feeling was one of overwhelming claustrophobia and of a lack of room overhead: Tom had almost to bend double as he made his way along past a tangle of pipes and gauges and electrical equipment. He and Brewster, with the German engineer, made their way aft through the battery room to the tail; then back again towards the torpedo-tubes in the bow. Four tubes, all loaded and evidently ready to fire. Other torpedoes, shining, lethal weapons, lay in the racks.

'Bastards,' Brewster said flatly.

'Brave men, though. I wouldn't fancy being depth-charged, shut up in a tin can.'

'Best thing for 'em, sir.' Brewster looked sourly at the German, who had been explaining the set-up as they had made their way through the boat. 'You,' he said to him. 'You and your mates. How many British seamen you bin murdering, eh?'

The man, plainly fearful of Brewster, shrugged. 'I did my duty, as did my friends, my shipmates.'

'For perishin' Kaiser Bill, eh?'

'It was my duty,' the man said again. 'You, too, have King George. You do your duty. There is no choice. We did not wish for war.'

Brewster sneered. 'Oh, no? You and your –'

Tom stepped in. 'Leave it, Petty Officer Brewster.'

'If you say so, sir.'

'I do say so.' Tom turned to the German rating. 'Are you a regular in your navy, or what we call Hostilities Only?'

'A wartime sailor only, *Herr Leutnant.*'

'And before the war?'

'I worked in Essen, *Herr Leutnant*, an engineer for the firm of Krupp. Before that I was in England . . . I took a degree in engineering, at London University. I came to know London well, and many other places also. I liked the British. I did not want the war. But like you, *Herr Leutnant*, I am a patriot. My duty was to help my country.'

Tom nodded; this was an educated man, caught up in the horror that war was becoming. Like hundreds of thousands of Britons, he would have joined up for reasons of patriotism and perhaps for an adventure, an escape from a humdrum way of life, again like all those hundreds of thousands of English, Scots, Welsh and Irish who to some extent had been as it were purblind, seeing a re-enactment of the South African war, a war fought mostly along gentlemanly lines, a war contained wholly within southern Africa, a war that had not involved civilians at home in danger as this current war might well do if the German zeppelins should ever darken the British skies with their giant helium cylinders and their bomb-loads.

The inspection completed, Tom made his way back towards the conning-tower hatch, sending the German to his former mess-deck where he would be under the watchful eye of Leading Seaman Harkness. Before climbing to the conning-tower Tom had a word with Petty Officer Brewster.

'He's a POW, remember. He's to be treated as such. Do you understand what I'm saying?'

Brewster looked belligerent. 'I understand, sir, yes.' He knew he had to be careful; there was something about Mr Chatto that said clearly that he wasn't to be messed around with, that he would take no nonsense from a PO or anyone else. But Brewster seethed beneath the surface. Bloody Huns . . . and this little bugger, what was his name, Kleberbaum – and there was a name for you – had been educated in England and then worked for bloody Krupp the armament manufacturer. He'd no doubt assisted in the production of the shells and bombs, the hand-grenades and rifles and machine-guns that were even now being used against the Allied troops in Flanders, and against the battleships and cruisers that were keeping the seas clear, standing between Britain and the bloody Kaiser and that von Hindenburg. And when Kleber what's-it, Baum or Bum more like, had been in London, what had he been doing? Spying most like, getting all ready to take a bite at the hand that fed him.

Brewster made his way along to the mess-deck. Leading Seaman Harkness was sitting on a bunk. So was Kleberbaum. Brewster aimed a finger at the German. 'Off your arse,' he said. 'Or should I say off your Kleber – bum.' He gave a cackle; Harkness looked surprised. The PO had never made what he thought of as a joke before, not in his hearing. '*Stand up when I speak to you!*'

Kleberbaum got to his feet and stood, shaking a little.

Brewster spoke to Harkness. 'Use the little swine to start cleaning up throughout. Boat's like a shit barge.' He paused. 'And you, Leading Seaman Harkness, just remember, you don't fraternize with the enemy, right?'

Tom chatted with Newman in the conning-tower as they kept a watching eye for anything hostile. 'Anything hostile' was most likely to be another U-boat – or its periscope. There had so far been few reports of any enemy surface vessels in the Mediterranean. Westerly, they wouldn't get through the Gibraltar strait: they would be blown from the water either by the guns of the fleet or the heavy artillery pieces mounted on the Rock. Easterly lay Port Said and the Suez Canal, with a big fleet presence not far off in Alexandria. A German excursion from that direction was also unlikely. But, as ever, you couldn't be sure, shouldn't make too many cosy assumptions . . . There was known to be a German naval presence in Turkish waters.

Watchful as ever as they moved along behind the *Geelong*, Tom's inner thoughts drifted on to other matters. There had been that letter from Grace Handley at Gibraltar; it had been short, very short, but it had shaken Tom and he'd been largely unable to get it out of his mind, at any rate when his duties and the recent action hadn't occupied him. Grace's message had been a shock: her husband, the 'dry old stick' who on the outbreak of war had been transferred to Admiralty service and appointed to Portsmouth dockyard, was ill. He was very ill. He had suffered a heart attack and had been taken to the Royal Naval Hospital at Haslar across the harbour from Portsmouth. The Fleet Surgeon in charge of the case had not seemed to hold out much hope. In the usual way of the medical profession he had not been precise; but there had been head-shakings, and pursed lips, and vague mutterings that had come to the same thing as a pronouncement.

Why should Grace write to Tom?

He was sorry for the husband, of course. But word of his illness . . . there must have been any number of matters other than writing letters on Grace's mind with a husband who was apparently dying. It was not as though there was any way in which Tom could help. Unless, of course, she'd thought he was in home waters with a chance of getting leave. He had not told her of his appointment, that he would be leaving the

UK. They had in fact parted on somewhat imprecise terms. Now, the fact that she had hastened – as obviously she had – to write to tell him the news raised queries in his mind. Did she see him as a potential husband? – that was his overriding thought. He had never thought seriously of marrying her; it had been she who had done the running, she who had talked, however inappropriately in view of her husband's position, of divorce. He had not touched upon the subject. But had he nevertheless encouraged her too far? Had he? He was fond enough of her; she had been a good companion and he had undoubtedly missed her when their meetings in Southsea had perforce come to an end.

But as wife? She was some years – not all that many, but some – older than himself. And she could be possessive; as an older woman that might become a weight on him. And there were other things . . . no, he didn't wish to marry her. He was not in love. But now, he believed, if the husband should die, there would be pressure. It was an unsettling thought, an unsettling situation to return to in due course. If he did return, that was; the war was as yet young. Those who had predicted an end by Christmas had been a long way out.

That night, with the Malta base now not far ahead, Tom took the middle watch in the conning-tower. The weather had eased; the surface was flat, the sky seeming alight with stars, great clusters of them hanging low to cast a brilliant sheen on the water. Trails of phosphorescence from the wakes of the *Geelong* and the submarine streamed astern. One day, when aerial reconnaissance on a large scale became another fact of war, those trails would be a guiding light for an enemy; but this night the two vessels moved ahead peacefully enough.

Vigilance was maintained to the full but it was also a time for reflection. With Tom in the conning-tower was Able Seaman Barrett to whom Fletcher had spoken on the night the floating mine had been sighted and who seemed to the

Captain to have something on his mind and to be in need of some sort of communion. In Gibraltar Fletcher had mentioned this during a conversation in *Cormorant*'s wardroom, he was very mindful of his ship's company's well-being. He had made the suggestion that Barrett might be drawn out a little and, if possible, helped or advised.

In the calm air of the Mediterranean night, Tom thought about this. He engaged Barrett in conversation in easy fashion. Barrett told him, as he had told Fletcher, that he'd been within a stone's throw of his transfer to the Royal Fleet Reserve and his pension. Tom followed this lead, asking a question similar to that put by Fletcher; and got a similar answer.

'I wouldn't really call it bad luck, sir, no.'

'You'd rather be afloat than on the beach?'

The answer was oblique. 'I've enjoyed my time in the andrew, sir,' Barrett said, using the lower-deck term for the naval service. 'I done my time abroad. Mediterranean, Bermuda an' that. China-side.' He paused. 'I was at the Taku Forts, sir, the Boxer Rising. Copped a bullet in me leg, got sent back to Hong Kong after the surgeon dug it out. All in the day's work I reckoned. Yes, I enjoyed my time, taking it all round. Be a bit on the dull side, ashore.'

Tom nodded. He would feel the same – if, say, married to Grace Handley and subsequently nagged at to leave the sea. It was never easy for a seaman to leave the sea; who wanted to employ someone whose qualifications, hard won as they might be, fitted him only for life aboard ship? There were other aspects as well: when a man such as Able Seaman Barrett, who had no doubt joined at the age of around fourteen as a seaman boy second class, left the service, he sacrificed free meals and accommodation, extra pay called subsistence when on leave, to say nothing of free medical attention, cheap tobacco, cheap clothing from the slop-chest, and an ordered life.

'Married?' Tom asked with a degree of caution.

'Yes, sir.' That was all; Tom decided to stop prying. If Barrett wanted to say anything about his married life, he would; if not – leave it. But it transpired that Barrett had more to say after all. 'Got a boy, sir. Coming up eighteen.'

'Following you into the navy, is he?'

'No, sir.' Barrett took a deep breath then spoke again. 'Conchie. Bloody conchie, would you credit it! Won't fight for 'is country, leaves it up to us old codgers to go and do it for 'im. Proud of it, 'e is. It's not as though there's conscription, not yet anyway . . . 'e 'as to flaunt it, announce what 'e'll do if ever 'e gets called up. It's mortifying, sir, that's what it is.'

Tom was embarrassed. What did one say to that? He said nothing, but believed he'd got to the root. To a man like Barrett, it would be indeed mortifying to live in the same house as a conscientious objector. Tom had heard disturbing stories of young ladies in London, society ladies, already handing out white feathers to men of military age who had not rushed to join Kitchener's Army to be mown down by the German machine-guns in the mud and filth of Flanders. Tom could himself see both sides of the argument: war had become a murderous mess, and he couldn't condone the white feathers. Some, according to what he'd heard, had been handed out by these spoilt, thoughtless damsels to men returned from sea or from the Front but not wearing their uniforms. Nevertheless, he could never be a conscientious objector himself and he felt much for Able Seaman Barrett.

As dawn came up, Tom was relieved by Newman and went below to the wardroom's constriction for a scratch breakfast. Leading Seaman Harkness had volunteered to be cook; he had an interest, he'd said. Stallybrass, when put aboard the U-boat for his structural survey, had found the galley storeroom well stocked, obviously for what had been intended as a long patrol, now cut short. Breakfast was fried eggs and sausages, not in fact very appetizingly prepared. It seemed that Harkness' interest did not translate into much ability. During his breakfast Tom became aware of a change in the U-boat's motion. She was lurching and heaving, which indicated a sudden change of weather such as could happen in the Mediterranean in winter. Newman, however, had made no report and Tom was reluctant to interfere until he did so. Newman, he had been told, was a permanent, peace-time RNVR officer and as such had done a year in naval service aboard a cruiser, with annual training periods with the fleet as well. From what Tom had seen of him aboard the *Geelong*, he appeared a competent watchkeeping officer.

But when Tom had gone along to the washroom for a shave, he felt the motion increase rather sharply. And when a call came down the hatch from the conning-tower, Tom left his shave half finished and ran for the steel ladder giving access from the control room where the periscope was housed. As he went he saw that there was already a slop of water on the deck of the compartment, coming down from where the plates had been damaged by the gunfire from the *Geelong*.

Reaching the conning-tower, he was met by a surprisingly strong wind, coming from dead ahead, from the east. Waves were curling over the bow, and water was streaming aft along the casing and washing up against the base of the conning-tower.

Newman said, 'I'm worried about the tow. The towing pendant's started lifting.'

Tom lifted his binoculars, hanging from a length of codline around his neck. He studied the towing pendant leading back from the *Geelong*'s after bitts. He saw it come clear of the water, come for an instant bar-taut, then drop back again. As it came up he had felt the jerk on the U-boat's bows. Then, on the *Geelong*'s upper deck, he saw hands moving aft under the First Lieutenant. As he watched there was a clatter on the ladder below him and Petty Officer Brewster appeared. Brewster took in the scene and said,

'Looks like the Captain's going to pay out more rope, sir. But I'd not worry about the tow if I was you, Mr Chatto. There's trouble below. Bloody Jerry's got himself a revolver.'

With Brewster behind him, Tom went down the ladder at the rush. The inquest could come later: someone should have searched the boat more thoroughly. The onus, he felt, was on himself.

Kleberbaum had taken his chance, apparently, when Leading Seaman Harkness had been clearing up after breakfast and had his back turned as he delved into the galley store. Kleberbaum had equipped himself with a concealed revolver when he'd been allowed to use the heads early that morning. One of the German crew must have stowed the weapon away before abandoning – possibly it had been Kleberbaum himself, which could indeed explain why the German rating had been a willing volunteer for return aboard. With Harkness' back turned, Kleberbaum had brought the barrel of the revolver down hard on his head and Harkness had gone flat out. Kleberbaum had now isolated himself in a midships compartment handy for the control of the diesel engines and the boat's electrics.

Brewster said, 'There's none of our hands behind him, sir, no dice that way. We'll have to attack him head on, I reckon.'

'Perhaps. First, I'm going to talk to him.'

'No use bloody *talking*, sir. Beggin' your pardon like. Shoot the bugger like a rat.'

'He's still a POW. If there's any shooting, it'll have to come from him first. In the meantime, I'll approach him alone.'

'Very good, sir.' Tom noted that Brewster made no suggestion that he might need support. He felt for his own revolver in its holster but did not draw it. He left the curtained-off wardroom space and went aft to the midship section and the battery room. Kleberbaum stood there, his face hard, almost wild, the revolver gripped in both hands and aimed straight at Tom.

'You will stay, *Herr Leutnant*. Not one step more, you understand?'

Tom halted. He said easily, 'For a POW, Kleberbaum, you're taking a big risk.'

'For my Kaiser, yes.'

'What do you hope to achieve? My ship is handy by and can use her guns the moment there's any trouble.'

Kleberbaum moved the revolver slightly. 'This guarantees that I am now in charge. Your ship will remain in ignorance until it is too late.'

Tom maintained his easy stance. He had an idea the German had gone a little off his head and it was necessary, if such was the case, not to precipitate anything. He said, 'You've still not told me what you hope to achieve. You're aware we're under tow, so you're pretty helpless. Aren't you? If you have ideas of taking over . . . I'd forget them if I were you.'

There was a sneer on Kleberbaum's face now. 'You think, perhaps, I have ideas of sailing the boat to a port where there is a presence of our navy. Yes, such exists in Turkey and beyond the Bosphorus. But that would be the dream of a madman . . . yes, that would be a madman's dream, *Herr Leutnant*, and I am not a madman.'

'Of course not. You're a patriot –'

'Yes, I am a patriot.'

'So just tell me. What is it you hope to do?'

Kleberbaum, still holding the revolver very steady, said, 'The boat will not be taken to Malta for the use perhaps of your navy against the German Empire. I intend to blow her up – and myself, and you British with her. I have the knowledge, and I have the means. I have the means all around me.' He jerked his head to right and left, towards the dials and gauges and pipes, the diesels and the batteries containing the acid that supplied the electric power and which, if spilled, would spread poisoned air throughout the submarine.

The prospect was a terrifying possibility. Tom said, 'You don't really want to die, do you, Kleberbaum? You have a family, I imagine. They'll want you to return when the war's over. To destroy one disabled U-boat is of pretty small use to your Kaiser . . . when you come to think of it. And thinking is what I suggest you do.'

The response was a laugh, a triumphant laugh. Kleberbaum had no intention of further thought. He held their fate right there in his revolver, in his skill and his professional knowledge of the submarine's potential. But there was a way out; Tom thought about that. He could gun the German down, getting the first shot in. Kleberbaum had probably prejudiced his POW protected status already. The legal right might be Tom's; but he detested with his whole being the idea of killing hand-to-hand, even though the German was certainly not helpless. Yet Tom had others beside himself to consider: Newman, Brewster, Barrett . . . his duty lay to them and he must not think of his own feelings, his own squeamishness.

Could he draw and fire before Kleberbaum? He blamed himself now for having left his revolver holstered. He would have to be fast, very fast indeed. He had scarcely begun to reach for his holster when Kleberbaum fired and then very quickly jerked his right elbow and all the lights went out, leaving an intense, impenetrable darkness.

TEN

THE GERMAN'S BULLET HAD GRAZED past Tom's right shoulder; the impact spun him round. He crashed into some of the machinery, fell to the coconut matting on the deckplates and felt blood run down his arm. He had no idea where Kleberbaum was but had not been aware of anyone moving past him towards the bow section. As he scrambled up he heard the sound of men coming aft: he heard Leading Seaman Harkness's voice.

'Here, Harkness. Watch out!'

'Are you all right, sir?'

'I'll survive.' Tom thought fast. He was in a dilemma; he knew nothing of submarines and neither did anyone else aboard – other than Kleberbaum. In the total darkness they would be able to do no more than fumble around uselessly, trying to isolate the switch that would restore the power, with Kleberbaum likely to fire blind at any moment. Tom had brought a powerful battery torch aboard the *Geelong*. This was with his gear in the submarine's wardroom but it would take some finding and they might not have much time left. Should he give the order to abandon ship, save his hands and let the U-boat go sky-high with Kleberbaum? And how far could he believe the German, come to that? Could a submarine be blown out of the water by some easy means, or was it all a bluff? Again, there was no answer. He heard more approaching footsteps, then Brewster's voice, a hoarse whisper. 'What's going on, eh? You there, sir?'

'Yes –'

'And the Hun, sir?'

'Somewhere aft, that's all I can say. He's threatening to blow the boat.'

'Well, now. Orders, sir?' Brewster sounded very much on edge, as well he might.

Tom blew out a long breath. Orders – they were all reliant on him. He had to give some sort of order. He came to a decision. Keeping his voice to a whisper he said, 'We need light. There's a torch if I can lay my hand on it. We'll move back for'ard, muster in the wardroom. If we have to abandon, we'll be handy for the hatch. And before long there'll be a reaction from the *Geelong*.' Tom was making the assumption, rightly as it turned out, that Newman in the conning-tower would have ticked over and sent a semaphore message to Fletcher – the power would probably be off the signal lamp. He said, 'Right, start moving. Slow and quiet.'

They edged along the deck. There was no sound of the German. They reached the wardroom and Tom felt around for his torch. He found it. He did not switch it on, but the feel of it was comforting.

Brewster asked, 'What now, sir?'

'For a start, I'm going up the hatch. I'll be back.' Tom moved away; as he crept for'ard daylight came down from the open hatch and movement became easier. The boat was lurching about in the worsening weather and there was more water slopping around from the base of the conning-tower. Climbing the ladder, Tom emerged into fresh air. He gave Newman an account of the state of things below; then saw that the seaboat was being lowered from the *Geelong*. He noted also that the towing pendant was riding easier following the paying-out of more slack from the towing end. With help on the way, he went back below to the mustered hands in the wardroom.

'Party coming across,' he said briefly.

'And in the meantime, sir? What about that Jerry, sir?'

'We wait for him, Petty Officer Brewster.'

'Suppose he blows the boat? He can do that any time 'e chooses.'

'Unless he's bluffing.'

'No *point* in bluffing, sir! Couldn't gain 'im anything, now, could it, sir?'

'Perhaps not. But I doubt if he really knows what he's doing in any case. His whole objective . . . well, it's pretty crazy –'

'Gone loony, sir?'

'Could be.'

'Even perishin' loonies can play funny buggers with the batteries,' Brewster said in a voice gone suddenly high. 'That I *do* know. Fumes, like. *Lethal* fumes.' There was a sudden movement and Tom felt Brewster brush past him. In the faint loom of light from the conning-tower Tom saw a figure making for the hatch. It was a case of Brewster first, evidently. Tom let him go; he would be brought up short by the party coming across from the *Geelong*, and thereafter he'd be sure to concoct a convincing yarn by way of excuse . . . Tom caught a muttered comment from Leading Seaman Harkness. 'All bull and no ballast.'

Then he heard Kleberbaum. There had been no warning sound but the German had crept right up close. '*Herr Leutnant.* Do not move. No one move. I shall shoot. Soon now the boat will be sunk. You will stay here and not escape. It is for my Kaiser and my Fatherland, *Deutschland über Alles* . . .'

He said no more. There was a tense silence. Tom's mind raced. Help was coming but only slowly across the disturbed sea. Kleberbaum had spoken of the boat sinking; not, as before, of being blown up. Very likely that plan had indeed been bluff, or had proved to be beyond Kleberbaum's capabilities after all. What did that leave? The answer stared Tom in the face: the sea-cocks, an opening of the valves that would let the sea flood in, a very different matter from the flooding of the ballast tanks when diving. And then, when the water reached the batteries, the killing fumes would come, spreading throughout the boat from stem to stern until the inrush of water filled her and took her to the bottom. Whatever happened, Tom knew one thing above all: the party of seamen from the *Geelong* must not be allowed to board.

A time to talk again? He said, 'Kleberbaum.'

No response. He took a risk; he flashed his torch, using his left hand well away from his body, his revolver in his right hand. There was no sign of the German. The man seemed to have the facility to move like a shadow, a ghost. And he was probably moving for the after flooding valves.

'I'm going after him,' Tom said. 'The rest of you, stand by the conning-tower hatch. Harkness – go up top and warn Mr Newman. Tell him, boarding party to lie off but be ready to pick us up.'

'You'll need help against the Jerry, sir –'

'No. We have no arms except for this.' He gestured with his revolver. 'Go for'ard – and hurry!'

As the ratings left, he moved aft. With his own lack of knowledge of submarines he had no real idea of where all the flooding valves might be situated, though on the early tour of inspection the German had pointed out one set of valves aft; there might be more for'ard but if Kleberbaum operated only the after ones that would be enough to take the boat down stern first.

Tom moved cautiously, not using his torch. He felt his hair rise at the back of his neck; at any moment a chance bullet might come, or there could be a sudden inrush of the sea, swirling along the deck, rising fast to the batteries . . . and then the fumes.

Inching aft, Tom heard a faint sound from ahead, a curious grating noise it seemed to be. Something being turned, some item of gear that was not responding easily? Flooding valves were certainly not something in everyday use . . .

Tom flicked on his torch. The beam wavered, settled on the German. Kleberbaum was turning a large red handwheel, his face contorted as the beam took him. Leaving the handwheel, he fired point-blank. Seawater was already starting its inrush.

As Newman in the conning tower heard the revolver shot echoing from below, he decided to ignore Tom's order for the *Geelong*'s seaboat to lie off. Coming alongside, the boat bumped hard against the casing; hands under Harkness took the lines and held the boat alongside for its crew to board. The First Lieutenant was with them. He called up to Newman, 'What's the state below? Where's Chatto?'

'He's below, Number One. He sent the hands up –'

'And the Hun?'

'Still on the loose so far as I know. There's just been more firing . . . I don't know what he's up to but we're beginning to lose stability, stern heavy.'

Stallybrass gave a nod, then turned to Leading Seaman Tubbs in charge of an armed party, rifles with bayonets now fixed. Cold steel, Tubbs reckoned, was always nice and effective – thrust it into a big German gut, twist, and withdraw, wonderful. Following the First Lieutenant's order, he led his party up the metal rings on the conning-tower's bulkhead, then down through the hatch, pushing past Petty Officer Brewster at the head of the ladder. Brewster had a surly look as though he didn't want to be spoken to, not that Tubbs wanted to make conversation anyway. Reaching the control-room Tubbs split his party up. 'You an' you an' you – move for'ard. Rest come aft with me, all right?'

They got on the move without delay. As a result of Newman's report by semaphore to the *Geelong*, it was known aboard that the electrics had gone off; Tubbs' party had brought torches. Tubbs was as yet keeping his party moving in the dark, circumspectly. They stumbled along in a rising slop of water, fending themselves off from machinery and pipes and electric cables, bumping their heads against protuberances from the deckhead. Tubbs felt his flesh almost literally creep as he advanced slowly in the lead of his armed seamen; the tension in the air was almost tangible. There was no knowing when the next bullet might come. Had the Hun got a reserve of ammunition, or hadn't he? In any case he'd presumably have a few rounds left in the chambers of his revolver . . . Tubbs sent up a silent prayer. He had a wife and children at home and they didn't need bad news, news of a nasty death in the bowels of a sodding U-boat . . .

On and on, slowly still, and all hands keeping as quiet as was possible with the jingle of rifle-slings and other equipment. The fixed bayonets were a dead giveaway, Tubbs reckoned, as they caught from time to time in those deckhead protuberances. Could have been a mistake, to board with fixed bayonets, but on the other hand those steel gut-puncturers could be a sight safer than blasting off with bullets that might go and set off something nasty, like an electrical fire or worse.

A sound ahead – or was it the imagination playing tricks?

Tubbs halted, putting out a staying hand to his next astern. 'Hold it,' he whispered. He felt the water deepening fast now around his legs, halfway to the knee, and the deck taking a more pronounced slope. Like Brewster, all he knew about submarines was the horrible potential of seawater reaching the batteries. He believed they hadn't much time left. The issue needed to be forced, brought to a head before they all perished.

But what to do? Where was Mr Chatto, what had happened to him? Maybe he was dead and the German was living yet. Tubbs felt the eeriness of their situation eating into him, maybe affecting his judgment. As a seaman, he'd never faced anything like this before. About to move on again, he caught another sound, louder and more positive than before. A protesting creak . . . like a valve being turned.

Coming to a decision, he flicked on his torch. There was a

body on the deck, seemingly dead. Aft of the body Mr Chatto, with blood pouring from his left arm, was turning a big red-painted handwheel. And he looked on the point of passing out.

Tubbs dropped his rifle to the deck and ran forward. 'All right, sir, I'll take over now.'

The U-boat was down by the stern but with the flooding valves turned off she would go no lower and the pumps would correct her trim. And the lights were back on again thanks to the *Geelong*'s ERA. With Stallybrass remaining aboard the U-boat to see it into Malta, Tom was taken with Kleberbaum's body to the *Geelong* and turned over to the surgeon probationer's care.

Dr Grant-Wylie reported to Fletcher on Tom's condition. 'Loss of blood mainly, sir. Otherwise intact now that I've removed the bullet. He'll be fit enough in two or three days.'

'Bighi?' Fletcher queried, in reference to the naval base hospital in Malta.

'I don't think we need bother Bighi, sir.'

Fletcher nodded. 'Right, that's up to you, Doctor. I'll need to see your patient as soon as he's fit enough. I'll have to make a report to Vice-Admiral Malta for transmission to the Admiralty.' He sighed; he disliked paperwork and disliked even more the kind of officious bullshit with which the Admiralty could plague seagoing officers when they felt like it – and this time they were going to feel very much like it. 'A dead prisoner of war, Doctor. Not funny. You've examined the body, of course.'

'Yes, sir. Death from gunshot. Bullet in the neck, severed the carotid artery.'

'Death instantaneous – not that that makes much difference. Death is death. And we know who fired the bullet, of course.'

'Yes. He told me . . . I'm not going to use the word

"admitted". Speaking out of turn if you'll allow me, I'd say he saved a whole lot of lives.'

'Amen to that,' Fletcher said feelingly. 'But the damn Admiralty's full of unbelievers.'

The *Geelong* entered Malta during the next forenoon. She came in slowly with her prize in tow, rounding the breakwater into the Grand Harbour with the armoured cruisers of the Mediterranean Fleet moored fore and aft to the buoys beneath the awesome shadow of Fort St Angelo, a centuries-old sandstone fortress that was once the home of the Knights of Malta and had been witness to Malta's long history of blood and war. As the disabled U-boat was seen and identified, men crowded the decks of the cruisers, watching as the *Geelong* proceeded to the berth allocated by the King's Harbour Master. As the two vessels moved past, spontaneous cheering broke out from the ships, from Fort St Angelo and from the Lascaris signal station, cheering that was joined by the Maltese civilians thronging the waterfront before the many-coloured shops and bars. A successful action against the marauding U-boats was a very welcome change from the far-too-frequent reports of the sinkings.

With his ship secured and the dockyard authorities making preparations to take over the U-boat and disembark the German prisoners for interrogation, Fletcher left the bridge and went below. Minutes later the yeoman came down to report a signal from Vice-Admiral Malta: '*You are to wait upon me at 1500 hours.*'

Fletcher caught the yeoman's eye. 'He's ticked over by the look of it. Seen the U-boat.' In wartime, wireless silence was not broken to make reports at sea.

'Yes, sir.'

'But he won't know yet about the dead German.' Fletcher went along to Tom's cabin. Fletcher had already got his story of events, but Tom was not yet back to duty. Fletcher told him of his summons to the Vice-Admiral. 'It's going to be like waiting outside the headmaster's study,' he said. 'And he'll almost certainly want to see you later.'

'A prisoner of war dead. That's bad, Fletcher.' The Vice-Admiral, who had turned out – fortunately – to be a decent old stick with a kindly, somewhat father-like face, was worried, no doubt with his own onward report to the Board of Admiralty in mind. He said as much. 'Their Lordships are going to have forty fits. Prisoners of war . . . not exactly sacrosanct, but certainly not far off.' He drummed his fingers on his desk, the hand protruding from a starched white shirt-cuff beneath the gold lace of his rank, a thick band surmounted by two thinner ones topped by the curl of an executive officer. 'It seems to me from what you've said that if your people had carried out a more effective search and found that revolver, then we wouldn't be faced with what we're faced with now. Agree?'

There could be no disagreement. 'Yes, sir.'

'Whom do you blame, Fletcher?'

Fletcher said, 'I take full responsibility, sir.'

'H'm . . . well, yes, as Captain. Do you wish to be more specific?'

'No, sir.'

The Vice-Admiral looked at Fletcher, hard, for some moments. Then he said abruptly, 'Well, I'll not press you. You've captured a U-boat – well done.'

'Thank you, sir.'

'God knows, we need good news. And your man – what's his name, Chatto. Full marks. It seems that he saved a number of lives by . . . disposing of the German in time. That can't be gainsaid. For myself, Fletcher, I approve the whole action. You can rely on it I shall put a good case to Their Lordships. In the meantime you'll let me have your written report as soon as possible.' He paused, then added, 'If you feel inclined to fudge a few details, so be it. I'll not probe. Taking account of all the circumstances . . . you understand?'

A wink was as good as a nod . . . Fletcher returned aboard reasonably satisfied. He lost no time in writing and submitting his report on the action and the subsequent events. And he added that in his view Temporary Lieutenant Chatto, RNR, was worthy of a commendation.

When Tom was summoned by the Vice-Admiral this view was upheld. But there was a note of warning all the same. 'There are certain aspects that may be raised by the Admiralty, Chatto. I'll ask you to tell me in your own words how Kleberbaum came to be killed.'

Tom's answer was straightforward. 'He fired, sir, as soon as I used my torch. He was opening a flooding valve. I fired immediately after, having been hit by his bullet. My shot killed him, as I discovered after the boarding party from my ship arrived.'

'The German quite positively fired first?'

'Yes, sir.'

The Vice-Admiral nodded. 'Killed, in effect, whilst attempting to escape.'

'Yes, sir.'

'But, of course – no witnesses. However, Chatto, I have absolutely no reason to doubt your word and I shall represent as much to Their Lordships.'

Happy words: but Tom left the Vice-Admiral's presence with the feeling that the affair was not over yet.

ELEVEN

BEFORE TOM HAD WAITED UPON THE Vice-Admiral, the *Geelong* had been shifted from the Grand Harbour to French Creek for repairs to be carried out as a result of the damage inflicted by the U-boat's gunfire. The repairs were expected to take a couple of weeks, maybe more. There would be a period of inactivity, but the island of Malta and its pleasures awaited the ship's company when shore leave was granted to the non-duty watch.

Tom went ashore with the surgeon probationer; they had grown friendly when Tom had been in Grant-Wylie's care. They crossed the Grand Harbour in a *dghaisa* to Custom House Steps, thence took a carriage to the catacombs, three layers of caves, grottoes and narrow passages excavated from the island's sandstone centuries before, largely for use as a burial ground. Moving along behind the light of a guttering candle held by their guide, they found heaps of bones still lying on shelf-like recesses off the passages. The silence, broken only by their own footfalls, was eerily oppressive; the total darkness when at one point the candle blew out in a draught was reminiscent of the U-boat. The candle was relit by a match to the accompaniment of vague mutterings from the guide who, like most of the Maltese, was barefoot, the soles of his feet as leathery as any boot.

'A lot of waste space around,' Tom remarked. 'Not much use to anyone. Or is it?'

'Food storage,' Grant-Wylie said. 'I believe they've been used for that in the past – grain storage. Malta's known quite a few sieges from time to time. The Phoenicians, Greeks,

Carthaginians, Romans and various other marauders . . . Vandals, Arabs, Normans, Turks. The island's had an interesting history.'

'You've studied it?'

'Not particularly, no. Just picked up a thing or two. I know someone who –' He broke off.

'Yes?'

'Oh, nothing really.' The girl who was carrying his child was something of a bluestocking, an undergraduate at Cambridge – Girton – when he'd been doing a stint at Addenbrooke's Hospital before joining the RNVR. She'd been reading ancient history. It was uncertain what effect her pregnancy would have on her continuance at Girton, but it was bound to be problematic. And Grant-Wylie didn't want to go into any of that. From the catacombs they went back into Valletta. The place was thronged with bluejackets, libertymen from the fleet, most of them making as it seemed for one place: Strada Stretta, that mecca of bars and brothels. For want of anything better to do, Tom and the doctor went along Strada Stretta, a street, or alley, of many steps, many smells and many goats, plus the odd priest flitting along in his black clothing and broad-brimmed headgear.

The very names of the bars were in themselves a commentary on British sea-power and on the servicemen that were in fact the mainstay of the Maltese economy: the Queen Victoria Bar, the Dreadnought Bar, the Lord Nelson Bar, the Invincible Bar, the King George V Bar, all of them packed with sailors.

'Just like Queen Street in Portsmouth,' Tom remarked. 'Only a bit more so, perhaps!' He glanced sideways at Grant-Wylie. 'Work piling up for you?' He indicated a big-bosomed woman, very dark and sultry with a flower stuck in her abundant hair, leaning from a balcony and calling out to the passing libertymen.

'Jig-a-jag, Jack, very cheap, very clean . . .'

Grant-Wylie shrugged. 'Some of them are bound to pick

up a dose, so I'm told. I'm not used to the ways of the navy yet but the Captain's warned me . . . he's going to set up a CDA mess if necessary.' He paused. 'Don't look now, but there's one possible candidate.' He nodded ahead. Petty Officer Brewster was seen to be entering what looked like a brothel, a side door standing open next to a bar, revealing a dark passageway and a sign in red lettering reading JOSIE COME STRAIGHT UP. Brewster took quick looks right and left and then saw the two familiar officers. He executed a quick about-turn and saluted.

'Ah, gentlemen. Just checking, sir, seeing none of our lads is doing what later they'll regret. Can't be too careful, sir.'

Tom kept a straight face. 'No, indeed, PO. You're absolutely right.' They moved on. When they felt it safe to look round, there was no sign of Brewster. He might not have entered the premises; on the other hand, he might. 'Even petty officers are human,' Tom said with a grin. Grant-Wylie said nothing; the whole business of sex was currently a sore point and no pun intended.

Bloody officers, Brewster was saying to himself as he dived in, didn't know why he'd bothered to cover his tracks really, no business of theirs, was it? And they all did the same thing, only posher.

Brewster climbed the carpetless stairs, grimly. He didn't go much on the surroundings but he had an urgent need and if he didn't satisfy it he'd go barmy. He'd waited a long time, a very long time. The missus back in the North Riding didn't participate much, once a leave if he was lucky. Always some reason why not: the usual headache, did he have to, or it was too cold. Or at times too hot. Of course there was Pompey, and China-side if you got a draft that way, but he'd never in fact been in the China Squadron and there were reasons against Pompey except when you were at your wits' end for a shag. The women in Pompey weren't up to much, scraggy, lank-haired, kids around, didn't show any enthusiasm, just lay back looking bored and wanted cash in advance.

But Malta was Malta.

They enjoyed it and let you know they enjoyed it. Really enthusiastic and full of ideas. Also friendly; home from home, if home had been like Malta, which it wasn't. Almost, you might say, a family affair. Petty Officer Brewster had done a number of commissions with the Mediterranean Fleet and he'd known Josie's mum, and her auntie too. It was going to be quite like old times, a chat over a drink of something, talk of the old days and how's your mum, and then wham.

Climbing the stairs to the sanctum, thoughts of Maisie suddenly crossed Brewster's mind. Back in Masham the night before he'd left for Pompey, he'd threatened her with the belt if she transgressed in his absence, not that she would, being Maisie and not keen, but it was a routine parting message, and anyway it was different for women.

'Long time no see,' Brewster said at the top of the stairs. He felt a pang of disappointment. Josie had definitely aged, no two ways about it. She'd sagged: stomach, chin . . . oh, well. Maybe next time he was out here she'd have a daughter coming along nicely. But in the meantime he was going to knock a bob or two off the price.

Definitely.

The day before the *Geelong* was due to emerge from dockyard hands a cruiser entered the Grand Harbour from Devonport with mail. For Tom there was a letter from brother Edward: the Dean had sunk into a kind of torpor, taking no interest in anything. Edith had visited him, but he'd seemed hardly to know her and had seemed glad and relieved when she'd said she must go (was Edward surprised at that?) and had avoided her attempted kiss (peck on the top of his head more like).

The news was unsettling if not unexpected. You couldn't uproot a man painlessly from almost his whole past.

No letter from Grace but, later that day, a cable. The husband had died. The funeral had taken place and Grace was remaining on at the flat. That was all.

What now?

What was he expected to do? He sent a cable back, expressing condolences. Nothing further.

Other items of unwelcome news reached the *Geelong* in that mail delivery. One such was for Mr Wenstock. His wife had died in the Portsmouth Royal Hospital, the death certificate showing stomach cancer. Mr Wenstock was shattered: he'd not been with the missus when she'd died. Well, you couldn't, of course, when you were serving overseas; but Mr Wenstock took that absence very badly. They'd been together for so long, then at the end . . . he thought of going to the skipper, requesting compassionate leave, but he didn't do that. The children were grown up, they didn't need him there, and in the midst of war you couldn't throw a spanner in the works by asking for a relief. He was indispensable to the ship . . . and, anyway, work was the best thing, keep his mind occupied. He didn't want time to think too much. So he got straight on with it, going along to the superintending shore engineer's office to make sure the various matters he'd wanted attended to had not been sidetracked in the usual way of dockyards.

Able Seaman Barrett also had news. Nothing fatal, but bad enough. His wife wrote to say the boy had been arrested for taking part in a demonstration against the war, right outside the main gate of the dockyard, on the Hard. Not just taking part: he'd hurled a brick at a police sergeant, the brick striking his head and knocking him out. The police sergeant had been taken to hospital and when the wife had last enquired he was still unconscious. The boy was due to appear before the Portsmouth magistrates the next Tuesday, and meanwhile was in police cells, no bail being given.

Barrett put his head in his hands, sitting there in his mess-deck. He almost wept. What a bleeding disgrace. His wife would suffer, he knew that. Pompey was a naval town through and through – the navy was everything to the townspeople, and they would react with catcalls and insults, maybe chuck a brick through the window of his little house off Arundel Street . . .

What could he do about it, stuck here in Malta, due to sail shortly on another U-boat hunt, to be another target for the Huns, while his wife went through a kind of purgatory, a hail of white feathers very likely? There was nothing he could do . . . he cursed savagely, reviling the boy but yet retaining a father's concern for a lad who'd been led astray by a bunch of yellow-bellied conchies. Nothing; or just one thing for what it might be worth: he could go to Mr Chatto to whom he'd already told some of the story. It might help, just to talk, though really there'd be nothing practical Mr Chatto could do.

There was more news of the war in the *Times of Malta* and in the London newspapers that had come with the mail. Bloody fighting in the trenches, a hundred yards gained here only to be lost again there under fresh German attack. A see-sawing kind of war, basically static in mud and dead men not yet buried. The casualty lists were lengthening all the time, names from every regiment in the Army List. A battalion of the Duke of Cornwall's Light Infantry had been virtually wiped out in the early days of the war, and this had been only the start of so many similar decimations. Already the regular battalions were thinning out, their replacements coming from the volunteers of Kitchener's army – the contemptible little army, according to the Kaiser. All keen enough – at first, anyway – but inexperienced, needing knocking into shape as fast as possible by what was left of the regular NCOs.

At sea the losses continued, one laden merchant ship after

another going down to the U-boats. There was an urgent need for more and more replacements from the shipyards that were working round the clock already. They would cope; but the seamen themselves were harder to replace. It had been said that it took a minimum of four years to make a seaman.

It seemed to be all gloom. Britain appeared to be staring defeat in the face. But that was something that must never be allowed to happen.

'Yes, I do understand,' Tom said. Barrett had come to his cabin, cap tucked beneath his left arm, obviously embarrassed and very formal, asking permission to speak. Tom had sat him in a chair and the two had faced each other, almost knee to knee in the small cabin with the port giving a view of the dockside. 'I understand your concern for your wife. People – mobs – can be frightening enough. Cruel, too.' He ran a hand over his face; he was as embarrassed as Barrett. What did you say to a husband, a father? The best thing was to say nothing, until perhaps more emerged. Just let the man talk, and offer a sympathetic ear.

'It's not that he was always like that, sir. Keen on the navy, he was, as a youngster. Used to wear my cap . . . you know the sort of thing, sir, I'm sure. March up and down with a stick over 'is shoulder, left-right-left.' Barrett paused. 'It's the company 'e got into, them conchies. Peace-lovers they call themselves. Last time home, I asked him what 'e'd do if the Huns attacked his mum.'

'And?'

'Didn't answer, sir. Looked dumb, insolent like. That was at first. Then 'e said, that was the sort of daft question the war-lovers always asked, just to try an' catch you on the hop like.'

'It's a real enough question.'

'I know that, sir.'

Tom asked, 'How does his mother feel about it, about his views?'

Barrett said promptly, 'Same as me, sir. Mortified, she is. An' she's *fond* of the lad. Sun shines out of 'is bottom. Even now. With 'im shut away, well, I'd not answer for 'er state of mind, that I wouldn't. I –'

'You think it may affect her health?'

Barrett nodded. 'I do, sir, yes. She's been poorly a while past. Her dad died . . . her mum's a worry, always wanting 'er round to help, do this, do that. Shopping and cooking and cleaning, bit o' nursing.' He paused, blew his nose hard. 'This lot, sir, the boy, well, it'll be the last straw.'

'Yes. I'm very sorry, Barrett. But I have to say there's little I can do. You probably realize that.'

'Yes, sir, I do.'

'On the other hand, I'll do what I can. Indirectly, that is. No one can interfere with the law . . . but I'll have a word with the Captain and then I'll see you again. In the meantime – no promises. Understand?'

'Yes, sir. And thank you, sir.' Barrett left the cabin; Tom believed he looked a shade easier. The Captain . . . Tom would speak to him, but had very little hope.

'What you're suggesting, Chatto, is a draft home on compassionate grounds?'

'Yes, sir. The man's worried sick, mainly, I think, on account of his wife.'

'It's understandable. He's taking it really badly?'

'Yes, very. He's going to have his mind on Portsmouth from now on. It could have an effect on his work, on his ability.'

Fletcher sighed. 'You know, Chatto, there's a school of naval thought that says a man – officer or rating – is wedded not to a wife but to the service and the ship. That he has no business to let his mind wander from that fact. That if he makes a balls-up and endangers life, he can't afterwards plead home worries.'

'That's a hard doctrine, sir.'

'Yes, it is. As a matter of fact it's one I don't condone. But neither do I wish to go to sea with someone who might not react in a proper fashion in action. A man with a grievance. He can become bitter, resentful.' Suddenly Fletcher grinned. 'You've presented a good case, Chatto. I'll make a signal to VAM requesting a relief – a replacement can be provided by Fort St Angelo. There's not much time left now before sailing, so I'll try to hurry it up in person – I'm going ashore to Lascaris, and I'll drop a word in the ear of the drafting commander.' He looked at his watch. 'Do me a favour, Chatto – tell the Officer of the Day to grab hold of a passing *dghaisa*. And Chatto – not a word to Barrett in the meantime. We don't want to have to dash his hopes.'

That afternoon the *Geelong* moved off the dockyard wall, the repairs completed and her bunkers full of coal once again. She moved out to a buoy in the Grand Harbour. Picking up a buoy was routine work, at least for experienced hands, but it was never particularly easy. Accidents could happen from time to time.

This was one of those times.

With the First Lieutenant in charge, and Petty Officer Brewster much in evidence, shouting the odds, the starboard anchor was detached from its cable and hung off. The seaboat was slipped and pulled ahead while the picking-up wire was lowered from the fo'c'sle through the bullring in the eyes of the ship. As the seaboat neared the buoy, lying just underfoot as Fletcher on the bridge nudged the ship up to it, the man detailed as buoy-jumper leapt nimbly from the boat on to the buoy, grabbed for the picking-up wire and secured it to the ring of the buoy. When the wire was fast, the buoy-jumper called up to the deck.

The First Lieutenant passed the order to the shipwright on the windlass below the break of the fo'c'sle: '*Hoist away!*'

The brake came off the windlass, the drums revolved, the picking-up wire came up bar-taut, lifting the buoy a little way from the water, taking its weight while the cable, free of its anchor and already partly paid out, was lowered further to be taken by the buoy-jumper and shackled on to the ring of the buoy. This was done; with the shackle secure, Stallybrass gave the order to lower away on the windlass, with the object of settling the heavy buoy back in the water.

That was when something went wrong.

As the brake came once again off the windlass, the buoy and the attached cable took charge, the links of the cable flying out at the rush amid clouds of red dust brought up from the cable locker below. And something very much worse: a yell of terror and agony as one of the ordinary seamen of the cable party was seen to fly through the air as though propelled from a gun. He fetched up against the bullring as the heavy links of the cable ground on through his body . . . fetched up a bloody, pulped mass of quivering flesh, the sounds of his agony ending suddenly in a kind of gasp. All hands stood stock-still for a moment, as though turned to stone. Then Petty Officer Brewster's harsh voice broke the spell.

'Daft bugger, must have got 'is foot caught in a link . . .'

Stallybrass swung round on him, his face livid, and never mind that junior ratings were present. 'Show some respect, Petty Officer Brewster, the lad's dead!'

Brewster flushed, but said nothing. He knew well enough that as the PO he should have been watching out for any such cack-handedness. Now all anyone could do was clear up the mess and hand the body over to the surgeon. Then arrange a funeral party. And something else, important to Brewster: slide out from under a possible charge of negligence. The First Lieutenant would get it in the neck too, of course, but only from the skipper in private most like.

Brewster was the one who had the immediate responsibility and he stood to lose his rate.

Brewster felt murderous. Daft little git, going and doing a thing like that.

Fletcher held an enquiry as soon as possible. Stallybrass admitted his overall responsibility straight away. Fletcher made the point that he was entitled to rely on his petty officer when his, Stallybrass', whole attention was properly on the buoy itself and he had his back turned. 'I'll see Brewster and the shipwright later,' he said. 'The first thing is to arrange the funeral. Full honours – guard with belts, gaiters and side-arms. Firing party. And I'll have to report to the Vice-Admiral. And write to the next-of-kin. The parents, probably . . . the chap was little more than a boy.' He added after a pause, 'Let's hope the ship's company doesn't see this as an omen. I think we all know what seamen are like.'

Later that day a signal was received from the drafting commander ashore in response to Fletcher's efforts to obtain a relief for Able Seaman Barrett: *Regret circumstances do not warrant relief on compassionate grounds.*

Fletcher swore. 'That's the shore people for you, Chatto. Anyway – tell him we tried.'

Tom believed the fact of a conscientious-objector involvement could in itself have had more than a little to answer for. At a time when men were breaking in battle and being put before a firing squad for cowardice, feelings were running high.

The burial took place the next morning, the sailing of the *Geelong* being delayed for the purpose. The body left the ship in a coffin rather than the man's own hammock as would have been the case in a sea burial. The coffin was lowered over the side to be taken aboard the seaboat together with the firing party and Lieutenant-Commander Fletcher and the sub-lieutenant who would be in charge of the cortege. Then the coffin, covered by a White Ensign, went ashore at Fort St Angelo, where it was placed in naval transport for conveyance to the burial ground by Bighi hospital.

Returning aboard after it was all over, Fletcher, who had already interviewed the shipwright who had operated the steam windlass the day before – there had been a defect, already made good by men sent across from the dockyard – sent for Petty Officer Brewster. He asked for an explanation.

'Cack-handedness, sir. Couldn't be helped, sir. Some ratings is like that, sir, as I dessay you know.'

Fletcher nodded. 'Had you given a warning to stand clear of the cable?'

Brewster had, so he answered honestly. 'Oh, yessir, course, sir. You can ask the 'ands, sir. Likewise a warning about wires lurking about.'

'You were aware the hands, most of them, were inexperienced?'

'I was, sir, yes.' There was caution now: could be a trap. If you knew the hands were green as grass, you took extra care. 'Hence the warning, sir. Kept an eye I did, sir.'

'Yet you failed to keep it at the relevant moment.'

Brewster stood silent, rigid at attention, his gaze fixed on a point a little above the Captain's head.

'Well, Brewster? How was that?'

'Dunno, sir. A lot to watch, sir. And it happened fast like, very fast. Lad was there one minute, gone the next.'

Fletcher was watching his face closely. The PO was an abrasive bully, unloved by the hands. But he was a good seaman all the same; and no man could have his eyes everywhere. It would be very difficult, and perhaps unfair, to pin blame. Brewster sensed the way the Captain's mind was working. There was something in the air that told Brewster he was going to be in the clear. He'd already been reassured insofar as the skipper had sent for him to hear his story. Normal procedure if he was to be put in the rattle for negligence or some such would have been for him to be brought up before the Officer of the Day and given First Lieutenant's Report for investigation, then Captain's Report for a decision. Well, that hadn't happened, and thank God for it.

Fletcher said abruptly, 'All right, Brewster. I'll be making a report to the Vice-Admiral but that'll be all for now.'

'Yessir, thank you, sir.'

Brewster turned about, replaced his cap and left the cabin. He hadn't quite liked the 'for now' but reckoned it would turn out all right. You couldn't chuck blame at a PO for not watching every sodding movement of an idle rating's feet. Not if you were in your right mind. Even if you were a vice-admiral . . .

When Fletcher's report reached naval HQ it was brought, since the *Geelong* was awaiting his sanction to leave port, to the Vice-Admiral's immediate attention.

He considered the matter fairly briefly. There were many matters to be dealt with, matters of more importance.

He looked up at his Chief of Staff. 'We don't want to delay the ship further, Fennimore.'

'No. She's needed off the Aegean. Needed badly. As you know, sir, the German Naval Command has increased its –'

'Yes, yes.' The Vice-Admiral shuffled papers on his desk. 'Damn bad luck – poor fellow! Some parents somewhere . . . but just one more burden of grief. I can't see that any one person is to blame. Defective windlass, wasn't it?'

'Yes, sir. Now repaired.'

'Well, that's it then, don't you agree? The engineer to blame in my view . . . but I'll not take the matter further, Fennimore. Mustn't delay the war.'

Had Mr Wenstock been present he would have said, that's right, blame the poor bloody engineer. But Mr Wenstock was not present and was in fact blaming himself. Steam on the windlass was his departmental responsibility and he'd already said as much to the Captain. But Fletcher had not cast blame. Windlasses, old ones especially, were tricky and unpredictable. Also, warrant engineers were not familiar with windlasses. Aboard ships of strictly naval construction there was a centre-line capstan rather than a windlass. Just the same, Mr Wenstock couldn't get it out of his mind, thinking of that lad's bereaved parents back in the UK. Such an unnecessary death.

As dark was coming down over the Grand Harbour the *Geelong* was slipped from the buoy, the cable was brought back inboard and shackled again on to the starboard anchor. When all reports had reached him Fletcher, on the bridge with Tom, put his single-screw engine to slow ahead, made his departure signal to Lascaris, and moved outwards for the boom and the Mediterranean night. Once outside the breakwater, Fletcher turned to the eastward, heading ostensibly for Alexandria, once again a target for the U-boats, her ship's company once more in their tramp-ship rig.

TWELVE

BREWSTER WAS SAVAGE BENEATH HIS cloth cap and ratty waistcoat. He knew he was unpopular with the hands; unpopularity was usually the lot of the efficient. Well, maybe he did drive the matloes a bit, but only because he had to. They were a pretty useless lot, unseamanlike, not long since the Hostilities Only men had been milk roundsmen, or butchers' delivery boys on bicycles, or clerks, or shop assistants or suchlike.

He was used to such landlubbers resenting him; but it was different now, ever since That Day. Thrusting eastwards into the Mediterranean – peaceful so far – Brewster sensed that he was being blamed by the hands for what had happened. He got looks; he overheard remarks. There was a surliness afoot when he gave his orders; it was almost as though they'd lost some of their fear of him – and why, he asked himself? He gave himself his own answer: *Because the buggers knew the officers had their eye on him.*

It wasn't fair. Brewster wouldn't let them get away with anything, though. He was the chief buffer and he would act as such notwithstanding.

That Barrett for one: Barrett was an active service rating, and he was a good seaman, knew his job from A to Z, didn't need much supervision let alone chivvying. Or – that *had* been the case. He'd changed since Malta. Sort of pissed-off look about him, and an air of not being with the ship, not caring any more. That would have to be watched; Barrett should be doing what he'd done until now, setting an example.

Brewster marched along the well-deck towards the fo'c'sle, arms swinging like a gunner's mate on parade. The cloth cap and the waistcoat didn't tally with the stance. He looked ridiculous; he heard a raspberry being blown from behind him. When he swung round there was only one man in sight: Leading Seaman Tubbs, grinning cheerfully.

'You make that sound, Leading Seaman Tubbs?'

'What sound might that be, PO?'

Such bleeding innocence! No proof, though. Brewster could end up being made to look silly. He took three paces towards Tubbs, coming up close. 'Watch it,' he hissed between his teeth. '*Just bloody watch it, that's all!*'

Looking up towards the bridge, Brewster caught Tom's eye. The look on the officer's face said that he, too, was watching something and not liking what he saw. Brewster turned sharply for'ard and resumed his march. He'd show 'em, oh yes, he'd show 'em all right, the sods . . . His mind flashed away from the ship on a wave of sudden nostalgia for Malta. Josie, now. She might have aged, but she was still a haven of pleasure and relaxation. Also she thought the world of him, she'd made that plain enough. He got *respect* from Josie. He consoled himself with that knowledge. He'd be back in Malta again before long.

U-boats permitting, that was.

Brewster had reached the fo'c'sle for a snoop when the telegraphs rang on the bridge. The thump of the engines increased. And Brewster heard his name called in a shout from the bridge wing.

The leading telegraphist had brought a message of urgency, a mayday call from a British freighter: the s.s. *Springwell*, torpedoed not far south of Crete. The ship's position as given was pencilled on to the chart by Tom. 'Around forty miles ahead, sir.'

'Three to four hours steaming.' Fletcher went to the engine-room telegraph and called the starting-platform.

'Emergency,' he said. 'I'll want all you've got.' That was when he called down to Brewster below on the fo'c'sle.

'Petty Officer Brewster.'

Cloth cap, no salute, but habit held. 'Yessir?'

'Don't salute – Mister! There could be a periscope trained on us. I'm steaming to the assistance of a ship that's been torpedoed. We should raise her in three hours. See everything's ready for getting away the seaboat – and have jumping ladders and scrambling-nets ready as well.'

'Aye, aye, sir –'

'And warn Leading Seaman Tubbs. I'll need the guns' crews on top line.'

Refraining this time from saluting, Brewster went off to shout the odds around the ship. On the bridge Fletcher conferred with Tom and the First Lieutenant. One likely problem might be the U-boat that had torpedoed the *Springwell.* If she'd picked up the wireless message from the sinking ship, she would possibly have made herself scarce by now. On the other hand, and much more likely in fact, she may have submerged to await any ship responding to the mayday call.

They were probably steaming into the lion's mouth; but the tradition of the sea left no choice. The sub-lieutenant was brought up to take over the bridge watch; Stallybrass went below to supervise the preparations for picking up survivors; and Tom, taking up his duties as gunnery officer, mustered his guns' crews and put them through their paces without, as yet, opening up the gunport doors. As ever, anonymity must be maintained until the moment of action.

Able Seaman Barrett was detailed as a lowerer for the seaboat. 'And look likely,' Petty Officer Brewster said. 'What you 'aven't bin looking of late. What's the matter with you, eh?'

'Nothing, PO.'

'Nothing, eh! Pull the other one. Go and get yourself a dose back up the Gut, did you?'

'No, I didn't. I don't go for that sort of thing.'

'P'raps you oughter, then, get the dirty water off of your chest. Talk about Weary Willie, your face is enough to put the cat off the milk.' Brewster moved away and Barrett breathed a sigh of relief. Let the sod go and be a pain in the arse somewhere else. Barrett looked at the fingers of his right hand. He had bunched them into a fist. Bunch of fives . . . that was what bloody Brewster was asking for. One day he just might get it. It would be worth a spell in detention quarters – DQs, in Pompey barracks. Wouldn't help the family situation, though.

Bugger Brewster; Barrett had those other matters to worry about. So had Mr Wenstock, as he nursed his old reciprocating engines up to a full head of steam by courtesy of the stokers sweating their hearts out in the stokehold, feeding the boilers under the stoker PO. The loss of Wenstock's wife was a sore wound that wouldn't heal. He dreaded going home the next time leave came around. Fortunately that was not likely to be for more than a year, perhaps two years if the *Geelong* wasn't sunk before then. Normal peace-time commissions in the Med had customarily been a two-year stretch, but of course things were changing with the war. But home, now; it just wouldn't be home any more. Not on his own. The children were grown up and married; they wouldn't live with him, nor he with them. In Mr Wenstock's view, the generations didn't mix, not in the same house they didn't. Stood to reason, did that; the old were set in their ways and didn't want change. But God alone knew what he'd do, all by himself, when he took his pension. Become a barrack-stanchion in the Crown and Anchor in Queen Street, most likely, tucked away in a corner nursing his sorrows behind a pint of Brickwood's, or yarning with old shipmates about days past, days when he was a young ERA 4, going steady with Edna and waiting for a bit of promotion before getting spliced. And not welcoming a draft chit to the China squadron. Mind, the Atlantic Fleet had been different, mostly in Pompey or Guz or Chats, interspersed with exercises when they went down to the straits for a while to join the Mediterranean Fleet for shoots and regattas and what-have-you; or went north to Scotland, to Invergordon on the Moray Firth, with the skirl of the pipes as often as not coming across on an offshore wind . . .

Memories, reveries, about all that was left. Mr Wenstock's current reverie was broken by the urgent whine of the voice-pipe. 'Captain here, Chief. *Springwell* in sight, stand by for engine manoeuvres.'

Any minute now. They were not far off Crete, where the U-boats had been especially active of late, according to the buzz in Malta.

Fletcher had raised the *Springwell* some eight miles off his port bow, the visibility being good. Through his binoculars he saw that the freighter was well down by the stern. He didn't believe she had long to go. Boats were seen, heading now for rescue. The ship had obviously been abandoned, no doubt after some loss of life.

Fletcher took his ship in at full speed. He was convinced that the attacking U-boat was lurking in the vicinity. He spoke to the guns. 'Mr Chatto . . . stand by to lower gunport doors, both sides to be ready for action.'

'Aye, aye, sir. All ready down here.'

'Good. Stand by for surprises.' Fletcher turned to the sub-lieutenant. 'Mr Lasenby, a very sharp lookout all round. Eyes skinned more than ever from now on.'

'Aye, aye, sir.' Lasenby lifted his binoculars for the hundredth time. Apart from the sinking freighter and the boat-loads the sea was empty. Empty and calm; it should not be hard to spot the feather of spray from a periscope. Lasenby was almost wishing away his sub-lieutenant's single gold stripe, wishing he was back as senior midshipman in the

Collingwood. Battleships had a safer life; they were well protected with heavy armour plate where the *Geelong* had none; and they had anti-torpedo nets and anti-torpedo bulges along their sides to take the first impact of an exploding tin fish. It was not easy to sink a battleship and her retaliatory gun-power was immense, shattering when she opened with a broadside from her 14-inch turreted guns.

Fletcher called down to the deck. 'Petty Officer Brewster – and don't salute.'

'Yessir – no, sir. That is –'

'All right, Brewster.' Fletcher felt inclined to add, Don't get your knickers in a twist, but refrained. 'Panic party all ready?'

'Yes, sir.'

'And the seaboat?'

'Will be, sir, soon as you give the word, sir.'

'Right.' The seaboat was still griped-in to the davit-head; nothing must be given away yet, revealed to the watching eye of a U-boat captain in his control room should he raise his periscope.

At the 4.7s Tubbs sucked painfully at a hollow tooth: should have asked to see the toothy at Fort St Angelo . . . too late now. Any road, a sudden cure for toothache might emerge at any moment from the placid waters of the Med. His name might be written on that tin fish, not a pleasant thought. Tubbs' ample gut squirmed a little. But on the whole he was fairly philosophical. War was after all what he'd joined for and if it happened, well, it happened, only way to look at it.

Bugger that tooth. Maybe the quack could do something. If he wasn't going to be too busy shortly with patching up survivors, wounded men.

They steamed on. Nothing happened except that they closed the torpedoed vessel . . . and watched the end come. The bows rose sharply as the sea flooded her aft. The mainmast and then the foremast broke off as they met the sea; then, with a curious roaring sound she went down fast, vanishing from sight, after which there was a muffled explosion followed by clouds of steam that burst through the boiling-up of the sea that marked her final death-agony. Just before the bridge superstructure went under, Brewster glimpsed a figure on the vessel's bridge. He didn't see him again. Probably the Master, staying with his ship right to the end. Brewster found himself breaking out in a light sweat. Some people . . . death or glory. It was in many ways better to be a PO than a ship's captain, RN or Merchant Service. The brass had that daft idea: the Captain was the ship, the ship was the Captain, one and indivisible. You went down with her . . . like that Captain Smith of the *Titanic*.

'*Stand by to pick up survivors!*'

The shout came from the bridge. The boats were close now. Brewster moved along the deck, where the Jacob's ladders and scrambling-nets were hanging ready over the sides. The survivors would have to climb up, or be helped up, wounded and all. There was no prospect of hoisting the boats inboard, there was no gear for that, no spare davit at least until the panic party was called away to bugger off in the seaboat.

'You all right, Barrett? Awake, are you?'

'I'm awake,' Barrett answered surlily. 'Let's hope you are.'

Brewster halted close. 'Insolence to a PO,' he said. 'Soon as this lot's over, you're up before the Officer of the Watch.'

Barrett said, 'Get stuffed.' But he said it under his breath. He felt murderous; he was being deliberately picked on. He thought of those yarns, of bastard POs being banged up in wash-deck lockers and jettisoned like the creeps they were. Just galley refuse, to feed the fish one day when their makeshift coffins rotted away.

Now the boats were coming alongside; and still no periscope. Maybe they would get away with it. The men who straggled out of the boats were the first priority now, though there was no lack of vigilance on the bridge. The survivors had not been long in the water; except for a number of burns cases and some wounds from the explosion, they were mostly in good shape. But those who were not were very bad indeed, as Fletcher, looking down from the bridge, saw for himself. Grant-Wylie was standing by with his sick-berth attendant as the wounded and the burns cases were helped up the scrambling-nets to the deck. There was a good deal of blood, many of the men with blood-soaked clothing, and some of the burns cases were screaming in agony as they were assisted, however carefully, aboard. They were then taken below in Neil Robertson stretchers to the ready-prepared sick accommodation. This was primitive, set as it was along the tween-decks, but it was the best that could be done.

There were twenty-seven survivors in all. When they were all aboard an officer wearing a torn and burnt monkey-jacket with three gold stripes on the cuff came capless to the bridge. He identified Fletcher: even in tramp-like garments, captains tended to look like captains.

'Thank God you got here,' he said simply. 'No one else seems to have answered . . .'

'Glad to be of assistance. You're the Chief Officer?'

'Yes. Thompson . . . the Captain remained behind. Wouldn't listen to reason. I –'

'Casualties – loss of life?'

'I'm afraid so. The torpedo hit close to the boiler-room and engine-room. It was a bloody inferno . . . they must have all died instantly. And a number of deckhands as well, caught in the blast.' His voice faltered a little. 'There was no warning, none at all. Just the explosion.'

Fletcher nodded. 'And the submarine? Did she surface after?'

'Yes –'

'Gunfire?'

'No gunfire. She could see we were done for, I suppose. No use wasting a shell on us. She submerged again almost at once, after that quick look around.'

Again Fletcher nodded. So there had been no attempt on the part of the German to pick up survivors. Well – that was more or less par for the course, except in some isolated instances where the U-boat captains had been more chivalrous. Fletcher felt rising anger as he heard the cries of the burns cases. He said, 'You may make use of my cabin, Mr Thompson. My steward will look after you . . . I'll be on the bridge for quite a while yet.'

'If you'll take my advice, you'll get the hell out, and fast. That U-boat's probably still around.'

'I expect you're right.' Fletcher grinned tightly. 'That's our job. You've not hoisted it in yet – and I take that as a tribute to our disguise. But we are an HM ship. A Q ship, hunting submarines. You may see us in action shortly.'

It was a grisly scene along the tween-decks. The injured men lay in the stretchers ranged along the bare wood of the deck. There was a smell of blood overlaid with the astringent smell of antiseptics. Grant-Wylie and his SBA had their work cut out. They moved from one case to another on a preliminary assessment to sort out the most immediate priorities. In some cases there were limbs to be amputated before gangrene could set in; but the surgery was primitive. Grant-Wylie, very nearly out of his depth but not quite, felt increasing nausea as he did his best to cope with the sheer volume of cases requiring his attention. He had never experienced anything on this scale during his student years. He and his SBA had to call upon the *Geelong*'s seamen for assistance: men undergoing amputations had to be held down physically in some cases, at least until the ether had taken effect, not always quickly. The tween-deck soon looked like a slaughterhouse. If only there had been nurses to assist . . .

'*Periscope bearing green four-oh, sir, distant three cables!*'

'Thank you, Mr Lasenby.' Fletcher brought up his glasses on the bearing. There was no mistake: it was a periscope right enough. Fletcher used the voice-pipes: guns and engine-room. At the gunport doors Tom and his guns' crews tensed for coming action. Leading Seaman Tubbs wiped sweat from his face with a hammy hand.

'Them poor buggers,' he said in reference to the survivors. 'They're going to get it a second time in one bleedin' day. Not fair, that.'

They awaited the next order from the bridge. That, or the impact of a torpedo – you could never rule that out; all U-boats didn't react in the same way. On the bridge Fletcher was also aware of this. He and the lookouts were watching for the submerged streak running through the water that would announce a torpedo on its way. If and when that was seen, the ship's head would be swung towards it so as to minimize the target area and allow the torpedo to pass harmlessly down their side.

But there was no torpedo.

Suddenly Lasenby reported, 'Periscope closing, sir!'

Fletcher had already seen it, and wondered what the next move was to be. Within half a minute there was a disturbance in the water, indicating that the U-boat was about to surface. Then the conning-tower broke through, streaming water from the washports, a cable's-length off the *Geelong* and half a point off the starboard bow.

The order went down the voice-pipe to the guns amidships. 'Open gunport doors starboard, fire when ready.' Fletcher turned to the Yeoman of Signals. 'Hoist battle ensign.'

As men began pouring from the U-boat's conning-tower and running along the casing for the gun, Fletcher turned the ship to port so that the starboard gun could bear, then waited for his own armament to open.

Nothing happened. Then there was a report from the gundeck. 'Starboard 4.7 misfired, sir.'

THIRTEEN

THERE HAD BEEN A TENSE MOMENT AT the open gunport doors when the 4.7-inch had failed to fire. Failed with a projectile up the spout, a nasty situation. Currently there was nothing to be done, according to Leading Seaman Tubbs. 'Best leave it, sir. We can't clear it in time.' In time before the German opened, he meant. Then, a moment later, they all felt the ship heel: the Captain, turning so as to present the port gun to the target?

But he wasn't.

There had been no time to manoeuvre the ship so that the port gun would bear. Something else had to be done, and done fast. Fletcher glanced at the bridge machine-gun crews, warned them to stand by, and then turned the ship to head directly at the German, once again following the principle of reducing the target area available to the U-boat.

Lasenby asked, 'Do you intend to ram, sir?'

'No. I'll use the machine-guns while she's got men on the casing.' He used a megaphone to call the machine-gunners and 4-pounder crews aft. '*Stand by to open!*'

He was not quite in time. In a split second the U-boat opened with its own machine-gun mounted in the conning-tower. The fire was accurate, and devastatingly so. As a hail of bullets swept the bridge, Fletcher fell, clutching at his throat from which blood was pouring. Lasenby, badly shaken, stared in horror then went for the voice-pipe to the guns. He reported the Captain wounded, maybe dead. It was Tom who took the report.

'Number One there?'

'No –'

'I'm coming up, sub.'

He ran for the ladders to the bridge, got the situation from Lasenby and took in Fletcher's intent. He said, 'I'll follow through as the Captain wanted.' He glanced down at the still figure lying in the bridge wing, felt nausea, looked away. The *Geelong* was coming up close now. 'Stand-by machine-guns port. I'll turn as soon as I'm close enough, then I'll steam down her side while the machine-guns rake the casing.'

He watched closely as the *Geelong* moved on; as the split second of timing arrived, he ordered the wheel hard over. The ship heeled, then steadied on her course, bringing the German parallel to her port side. On Tom's order the machine-guns opened, giving a raking fire right along the casing from aft to for'ard. The conning-tower personnel dodged down but the fo'c'sle gun's crew were caught in the hail of bullets, caught and colandered, their bodies falling to the steel casing and then sliding over into the water.

As Tom brought the *Geelong* round preparatory to another firing run, the U-boat was seen to be submerging.

Round one to the *Geelong*. But no one doubted that the U-boat would mount another attack as soon as she was ready.

Stallybrass, First Lieutenant, had been aft when Fletcher had been hit. The sudden heel of the ship had caught him off balance and he had slipped on the poop-deck ladder, falling heavily. He lay with a leg curled beneath him, tried to drag himself along the deck towards the bridge. He was in intense pain. The leg was probably broken. As he struggled along, sweat pouring from his face, Tom on the bridge saw that the U-boat was surfacing again, some 2000 yards off the *Geelong*'s port side.

He passed the word down to Leading Seaman Tubbs. 'Open when your sights come on, Tubbs.'

Petty Officer Brewster appeared on the bridge. 'Panic

party, sir?' Then he saw the Captain's dead body lying below the bridge screen. 'Oh, my God!'

How thick could you get . . . 'Too late for the panic party,' Tom said, 'I believe the U-boat's run out of torpedoes, otherwise she'd have used one by now.'

There was a crash from below as Tubbs opened with the port-side 4.7 and another loud report as the 4-pounder fired from the poop. Smoke billowed; then there was a flash from the U-boat, her gun manned by a fresh crew. A shell whistled over the bridge; another smashed into the poop with devastating effect. Fire was seen, flickering redly through the smoke. Tom said, 'Hoses – fire and damage control parties aft!'

Brewster slid fast down the ladder. Then the *Geelong*'s fire took its effect: the German's gun fell silent, and Tom's binoculars showed a red glow on the casing and no one left alive. The glow extended to a furnace and was followed by an explosion that rang across the water. A thick pall of smoke billowed out. Another shell from the 4.7 took the casing aft of the conning-tower, and the U-boat slewed under its impact. Another shell exploded on the top of the conning-tower.

'Cease firing!'

The gun lay silent. There was a curious silence over all, a silence like death. It was broken by the sub-lieutenant. 'She's going.'

Tom nodded. The U-boat canted stern down, her bows rising sharply. She hung there for a long moment, then slid down and away into the depths.

Tom felt a sense of awe. All those men, brave men who had done their duty, sliding helplessly beneath the Mediterranean. Tom believed there would be no survivors. But he waited on the off-chance. Waited, but kept way on the ship in case other submarines should be in the vicinity. If there were, they did not attack. And there were no survivors. Just debris coming to the surface after a while: shattered woodwork, items of clothing, oil. Oil in great quantities.

Tom looked down at Fletcher and then scanned the decks below. 'Where's the First Lieutenant?'

There was no answer until Petty Officer Brewster came aft to report the fire parties gaining control on the poop. 'First Lieutenant, sir. Caught in the explosion aft.'

'Bad?'

'Very bad, sir. Doctor's with him now.'

Leading Seaman Tubbs reported the starboard-side 4.7 out of action indefinitely. 'Job for the gunwharf, sir – dockyard job.'

'What's gone wrong, Tubbs?'

'Defective part, sir. All right till it gave up the ghost, like. Worn, rather than defective, strictly speaking, sir. Those guns, they've come out of worn-out cruisers bound for the scrapyard. You use what you can get, till the factories get going proper.' He added, 'Can't fire as it is, sir.'

'That's positive?'

'Yes, sir.'

'And the projectile?'

'Still up the spout, sir. I waited as per drill-book, sir, thirty minutes after a misfire before you opens the breech. Shell jammed fast, sir.'

'Safe to leave it?'

'Safer than to try to prise it out, sir. It won't go up, sir, not unless it cops it from a Jerry shell.'

It was dawning on Tom that in the absence of Fletcher and Stallybrass the command had devolved upon himself. It was he, now, who had to make the decisions . . . He told Tubbs to keep the useless gun doused with seawater as a precaution against possible explosion. He would examine it as soon as possible. Then he took a look at the chart. Until Number One was fit, and that might be a very long time ahead, he had to decide where to take the ship. With the necessity of maintaining wireless silence at sea in wartime, he was unable to ask for orders. The decision was his alone.

There was little point in remaining at sea with one gun useless and damage aft. And there were the survivors of the *Springwell* to be considered. So make for port. His nearest was Port Said, 400 miles south-easterly.

He sent down for the RNVR lieutenant, Frank Newman, to take over the bridge. Relieved, he went below to see Stallybrass, who had been removed to his cabin. Grant-Wylie, looking tired and anxious, was with him. Stallybrass lay inert, his face bloodless, his head, right leg and both arms heavily bandaged. He seemed scarcely to be breathing.

Tom asked, 'Well, Doctor?'

'I doubt if he'll make it.' Grant-Wylie looked up. 'I need hospital resources, badly. Not just Number One. D'you know where we're heading – and how soon we'll get there?'

Tom was about to answer when Grant-Wylie stiffened. There had been a curious sound from Stallybrass, a kind of coughing sigh, an exhalation of breath as it seemed, followed by stertorous, rattling breaths.

Grant-Wylie said, 'Cheyney-Stokes.'

'H'm?'

'Means he's going.'

Tom looked down sadly, then pulled himself together and left the cabin for the bridge. There were many things to be done now. Within the next half-hour, the voice-pipe from the wardroom whined. The bridge messenger answered and reported: 'Doctor, sir. First Lieutenant, sir. He's dead.'

Brewster was on the bridge, with a report from the shipwright: the hull was intact, all the damage confined to the superstructure aft. Hearing the bridge messenger, he said, 'Leaves you in command, sir, does that.'

'Correct. And Mr Newman will be First Lieutenant.'

Tom went to the chartroom to lay off a course for Port Said. Brewster left the bridge, hissing through clenched teeth. Mr Chatto and Mr Newman, the ship's company's lives in their hands and neither of them been in naval service a dog watch. And maybe fifty perishing German submarines between them and the safety of the land, wherever that might be. Malta, with any luck. Brewster had another moan later when the buzz said they were bound for Port Said. Port Said was a cesspit, smelly and flea-ridden, full of camels and gippos, and as for the women – cor! Not to be touched with a bargepole, let alone anything else. Poxy lot – literally.

Four hundred sea miles to Port Said: at the *Geelong*'s speed, it should take about thirty-three hours if the weather held. And if they met no more U-boats, or even German surface ships coming down from Turkish waters to harry British shipping passing to and from the Suez Canal. Plenty of homeward-bound vessels came through the canal, bringing vital supplies from the Empire – from Australia and New Zealand principally. But the possibility of attack lay in the realms of surmise. Other things were more immediate, such as the well-being of the *Springwell*'s survivors. And then there were the sea burials: Fletcher, Stallybrass, three of the survivors who hadn't made it despite Grant-Wylie's superhuman efforts – and there could be more before they reached Port Said. Stopping engines briefly and dangerously, Tom stood at the salute as, after he had read the brief committal service, the canvas-shrouded bodies were slid into the Mediterranean from the tilted plank beneath the White and Red Ensigns as appropriate to each. Thompson, the *Springwell*'s Chief Officer, stood at Tom's side. Tom expected to remain on the bridge for most of the way through to Port Said: Thompson would have the use of what was now his cabin. And that was where they both went after the sea burials. Each badly needed a drink: one small whisky apiece. It helped matters along quite a lot.

Brewster didn't waste any time. Barrett was marched to the bridge by Petty Officer Popplewell – Brewster could scarcely, as the injured complainant, present the case himself. So Popplewell brought Barrett up the ladder to be dealt with by the Officer of the Watch, who happened to be Sub-Lieutenant Lasenby.

'What's all this?' Lasenby asked.

Popplewell saluted. 'Defaulter, sir.' He addressed Barrett. 'Atten – *tion*. Off – cap. Stand *still*.' That was a routine order, even when the defaulter was as still as a rock and his cap was in fact a knitted woolly object. 'Able Seaman Barrett, sir, did offer impertinence to Petty Officer Brewster his superior officer, sir.'

'I see.' Lasenby turned to Brewster, lurking in the background, to give his evidence. 'Petty Officer Brewster?'

Brewster stepped forward and saluted. 'Yessir. The accused, sir, did utter certain words, sir, the words being, let's hope you are. The reference,' he added, seeing Lasenby's blank look, 'being to what I'd just said myself, like, to wit, sir, awake are you.'

'I see.' Plainly, Lasenby didn't see but discipline depended on the petty officers. 'Can you elaborate, Petty Officer Brewster?'

'I can, sir. Them words, sir, was said in a funny manner, sir.'

'Funny?'

'Like sarcastic, sir. Insolent intent, sir, if you follow my meaning, sir.'

'Yes.' This was a confounded nuisance when there could be U-boats around, but of course the discipline aspect was very important, especially in wartime. 'Barrett?'

'Sir?'

'Have you anything to say?'

Barrett's feeling were fairly mutinous. He knew Brewster was out to get him; knew that whatever he said now Lasenby was virtually bound to give him First Lieutenant's Report, which meant Captain's Report next. And the officers always backed the petty officers. A feeling of what-the-hell came over Barrett, still worried sick with home matters. Sod it all, he thought, may as well speak my mind, why not? It'd give him some satisfaction any road.

He said, 'Yes, sir. I did say that.' He paused, staring at Brewster. 'Said something else as well.'

'Go on, Barrett.'

'Yes, sir. I said get stuffed, sir.'

Brewster's face was a picture. Lasenby repeated, 'Get stuffed?'

'Yes, sir. Only the PO didn't hear that, sir.'

Lasenby kept a straight face. He nodded at Popplewell and said the expected. 'First Lieutenant's Report.'

Popplewell went into action again. 'First Lieutenant's Report, on cap, salute the officer, about turn, double march, down the ladder.'

What a farce at a time like this, Lasenby thought.

There would be repair facilities at Port Said, according to the warrant engineer, but very likely they wouldn't be up to much. The ship, however, was seaworthy and the most important consideration now was hospitalization for the wounded men. They could be landed to the military hospital in Port Said.

The run through to Egyptian waters proceeded without incident. Barrett was paraded at First Lieutenant's Request-men and Defaulters, he being in fact the only defaulter, and as expected was placed in the Captain's Report. When Barrett was brought before him, Tom dispensed justice in such a way that saved Brewster's public face but didn't do Barrett any harm.

He said, 'You'll know we're bound for Port Said, Barrett.'

'Yes, sir.'

'Looking forward to going ashore there?' He looked Barrett squarely in the eye, and gave a fractional wink. Barrett got the hint nicely. He had a shrewd idea that Mr Chatto knew very well indeed that he didn't give a toss for

Port Said, all he wanted was Pompey, to be with the missus. He said, 'Yes, sir.'

Tom nodded. He said, 'Seven days' leave stopped.'

But he didn't believe he'd entirely fooled Brewster, who stomped down the bridge ladder, his back view managing to convey hurt indignation. He was seething inside. Seven days' bloody useless leave stopped, for insolence to a PO! Should by rights have lost his good conduct badges, which would have meant a continuing loss of pay. Going aft along the deck behind Barrett he said harshly, 'I'll get you yet, don't you think otherwise.' Barrett half turned, fists clenched, then thought better of it. You couldn't win, couldn't buck the system in which you were always in the wrong. And the skipper had been pretty decent. You couldn't chuck it back at him by smashing in a petty officer's ugly phiz.

FOURTEEN

THE *GEELONG* CAME PAST THE DE Lesseps statue and the lighthouse, entering Port Said Roads in the fast-falling dusk. There was an undoubted thrill, a satisfaction in command, in for the first time bringing his own ship into port, though this was dulled for Tom by the circumstances that had brought it about. Other men's misfortune . . . The ship was directed to an anchorage clear of the traffic entering and leaving the Suez Canal. Decisions would be made next morning, when Tom made his report to SBNO, the Senior British Naval Officer. Once that report had been made, an inspection of the damage would take place. There was, however, no delay in the landing of the cot cases to hospital. A tender came alongside shortly after the *Geelong* had anchored and, with Grant-Wylie in attendance, the men were put aboard and taken inshore.

Next morning Tom went ashore to the office of SBNO. Arrangements were made for dockyard repairs to begin as soon as possible, which in Port Said might mean anything. But Tom made a strong case for priority – every Q ship possible was needed at sea. Time in port was time given to the U-boat commanders. Tom knew he was teaching his grandmother but it had to be said. The staff needed a kick in the pants. He did, however, learn something interesting: there was a hint, no more, that the *Geelong*'s operational area might be altered. Which left him wondering: would they be ordered through the canal and into the Indian Ocean to operate from some port such as Kilindini or Durban?

Making his way back to the ship, Tom strolled through

dirty, crowded streets. The port seemed to be full of troops of the Indian Army, Sikhs and Mahrattas and Punjabis. When he'd last been at home he'd heard via his brother Philip that there had been a good deal of military movement within the Empire; that Indian troops were being sent to Egypt and replaced on their own territory by British battalions from such stations as Singapore, Hong Kong and the Chinese mainland. Currently, the Indians swarmed everywhere, mingling with British troops in their khaki, with seamen and civilians both British and native, the latter in their red fezzes and flowing robes like dresses. Beggars, too; they left no one unmolested. And the busy pimps, the small importunate boys with big sisters.

'You like my sister, she very good, very versatile, very cheap, you come with me . . .'

Tom brushed them aside impatiently. He found himself in the establishment of Simon Artz, an emporium where almost anything could be bought, from a fly-swatter to a camel. It occurred to him that he might find something to take back for his father, when one day he got home leave. For Grace Handley as well, perhaps? Handkerchiefs, scent, a silk scarf? He was not much of a hand at shopping. He bought a hookah for his father, more as a joke than to be taken seriously. For Grace he bought a silver scarab, wondering if in fact he would ever see her again to deliver it.

Outside the store, he met Petty Officer Brewster going in.

'Good morning, Brewster. Present for your wife?'

'Not exactly, sir, no. The pong.'

'Pong?'

'Yes, sir, pong. You'll have noticed it I'm sure.' In fact Tom had; Port Said stank like a drain. 'Cleaner air in Simon Artz. Not a present for the wife, sir, no. By 'eck, sir, if I bought the old – if I bought the wife a present every time I got 'ome from foreign, why, I'd be bankrupt ten times over, sir.'

Tom moved on while Brewster sought his fresher air. Well, he thought, it takes all sorts.

The mail, seamen's friend and sometimes seamen's foe, arrived two days later. There was one for Brewster, from his wife, who didn't often write. She found it hard labour, putting pen to paper. This one brought solemn news: Mrs Satterthwaite had died, or, more accurately, had been killed. Run over by a bus in Leeds. Mrs Satterthwaite was Petty Officer Brewster's mother-in-law. Reading this news in the petty officers' mess, Brewster said, 'Bloody 'ell' and rummaged for a bottle concealed at the bottom of his locker; Brewster bottled his tot at sea and never mind that he'd run an AB in for the same crime back in the *Cormorant* huts in Gibraltar. He took a suck, then another, lovely. Popplewell entered the mess, saw him at it – but it didn't matter, he did the same thing himself.

'Birthday?' Popplewell asked.

'Sort of. Rebirth, like.' Brewster paused, then released good news. 'Ma-in-law pegged out.' He re-stowed the bottle. Cause for celebration or not, he saw no reason why he should give Popplewell any of his tot.

Another recipient of news was Able Seaman Barrett, whose worst fears were confirmed by a cutting from the Portsmouth *Evening News*. His son had been up before the bench and passed on to quarter sessions in Winchester for trial. In the meantime, he was held in custody. The *Evening News* reporter had had a field day: conchies were not popular, especially in a naval town where almost every household had someone in the navy, and all too many of them were mourning losses at sea. There was a bit about himself, Able Seaman Barrett, the father, serving his King and country at sea, and in danger. What a son to have, was the unwritten suggestion. Worse than anything – apart from the disgrace itself – was the fact that Barrett's address had been given. There were no reports of any bricks through windows – yet. But although the missus was keeping a stiff upper lip in her letter, so as not to worry him further, Barrett knew just what she would be going through. Neighbours, friends even, were not always very nice.

A draft home . . . might be worth trying the skipper – Mr Chatto now – once more? But no, he wouldn't bother the skipper. The shore people here in Port Said would be no more understanding than those in Malta.

There was mail for most of the ship's company and, as it happened, most of the news was bad. Dr Grant-Wylie's girl was being given hell by her parents; and the medical people were tight-lipped too, her own doctor and the nurses. Pregnancy outside wedlock was about the worst crime that could be committed and the victims, if that was the word, were to be vilified and despised. Grant-Wylie's heart bled for the girl. She needed his support, his presence, desperately. But an illegitimate pregnancy would get no help from the navy. Any such request would be precisely the sort of thing that made admirals bust guts, throw their brass-bound caps on the deck and stamp on them. Grant-Wylie, although new to the service himself, had a retired admiral for a grandfather.

The mail for Tom brought nothing further from Grace Handley: in that there was both relief and disappointment. His mind was as yet unclear about Grace. But a letter from Ireland brought deep sorrow. It was from Edith; brother Philip had been killed on the Western Front, along with a horrifying number of his battalion of The Connaught Rangers, going over to the top into no-man's-land in a push against the German front-line trenches. Philip, the eldest brother, had been Tom's boyhood hero. Tom put his head in his hands. It was all such a waste . . . Edith's letter went on to say that the Reverend Edward was arranging to join up as an army chaplain, news that Tom found rather surprising. The sudden valour was perhaps a gut reaction to Philip's death; or maybe God had told him where his duty lay. It had to be something of that sort, Tom believed, to drag Edward away from the coat-tails of his Bishop. But he wished him well, even though his absence on active service would leave their father to the mercies of Edith. Tom wondered how the old man would be taking the loss of Philip. With any luck, he wouldn't have taken it in. In her letter Edith had said – mentioned in passing really – that he'd just nodded at the news.

As soon as Tom had the time, he would write letters.

While the damaged poop-deck was being repaired and the defective 4.7-inch gun was being stripped down ashore, there were opportunities for leave. Tom and Grant-Wylie went ashore together, taking an overcrowded train to Cairo for an afternoon's sightseeing that ended in the bar of Shepheard's Hotel.

Grant-Wylie had three double whiskies in quick succession. He grew morose. Tom asked what was the matter.

'Oh, nothing. The war, I suppose.'

'The casualties?' Grant-Wylie had really been chucked in at the deep end recently.

'That and other things. Things that the bloody war doesn't exactly help.'

Tom nodded. 'Want to talk about it, Doc?'

'Not really.'

The tone was unconvincing. Tom spoke rather diffidently. 'It does help. And . . . well, I hope this doesn't sound pompous or – or anything like that . . . but as an unexpected and probably very temporary CO, it's my job to –'

'To run an efficient ship and ensure that private worries don't balls things up?'

'I suppose you might say that, yes. But –'

Grant-Wylie gave a lopsided smile. 'Sorry, old man. That was rude of me. I apologize. But the fact is, I *have* ballsed things up. Back in Blighty.' He finished his drink, called for refills. Then he said abruptly, 'Got a girl – *my* girl, not just any girl if you follow . . . got her pregnant. And I'm out here in bloody Egypt.' The whole story came out, the parents' attitude, the doctor's. Tom understood the anxieties but there was a part of him that said Grant-Wylie had been a bloody fool to put it mildly, and had shown a surprising irresponsibility for a medical man. This, of course, he couldn't say. Grant-Wylie said it for him.

'I suppose you think I've acted like a cad.'

'I –'

Grant-Wylie laid a hand on his arm. 'No – don't say it. I've been wallowing in self-blame long enough. But in a way it's the war that's making me the cad I never meant to be. What I mean is, I'd have married the girl if I'd known in time, before joining the ship.' He paused, glanced up with no hope in his eyes. 'What would the chances be . . . of getting sent home?'

Tom shook his head. 'I don't know the ways of the navy all that well yet,' he said, 'but they talk a lot about what they call the exigencies of the service. That covers a whole lot of things. I'd say your chances would be nil.' He paused, frowning. Shepheard's Hotel was a very cosmopolitan place, as was Cairo itself. There would be Germans around, possible spies, enemy agents . . . One of the ground-in precepts of his brief naval training period had been that you never, absolutely never, spoke in public of service matters. So such knowledge as he had been given, no more than a hint really whilst he had been discussing repairs and allied matters with the staff in naval HQ, must not be revealed. But he felt it safe to say, 'I wouldn't worry if I were you, Doc. Funny things can happen in war. Just a word to the wise.'

Leading Seaman Tubbs' toothache had worsened after the arrival in Port Said. He'd taken it to the quack, and the quack, diagnosing an abscess, had lanced it as a temporary measure and had then made arrangements for Tubbs to go ashore to a dentist. The dentist was a civilian, accredited to the navy to carry out dental work in the absence of a naval dental officer; and he was what Tubbs called a wog, very black, very smelly –

garlic – and none too clean. Tubbs had regarded the whirring, foot-operated drill with horror; likewise the other instruments of torture, steel scrapers and probes and things like pincers. An extraction had been needed and that meant gas; and gas meant the attendance of a doctor, also a civilian, also a wog, blackish and garlicky and with teeth the colour of his face, no advert for his mate the toothy. However, the operation had gone all right, leaving Tubbs grateful enough but hoping he hadn't picked up any terrible diseases. It also left him with a sore mouth and a swollen face as he tottered away from the toothy's shop, or surgery.

Best cure?

Need a bloke ask? Booze, of course.

Leading Seaman Tubbs, back in uniform now with the fouled anchor of his rate shining from his left arm, found a boozer. He was due back aboard, supposed to be, after his visit to the toothy. But what the hell! He'd had a hard time the last few weeks, what with one thing and another, bloody defective gun letting him down at the wrong moment, bloody discomfort aboard the ship – Tubbs much preferred his hammock to a bunk, a hammock swayed with the roll of the ship and didn't chuck you out on to the deck when there was an exceptionally heavy roll – and that bastard Brewster who seemed to think he knew all about gunnery as well as everything else to do with the service. Tubbs had also seen the way the PO kept on getting at Barrett. Thinking lurid thoughts about what he'd like to do to the slimy sod, Tubbs put in some steady work on the booze. He wasn't sure quite what it was, but it tasted like aniseed and it was good enough stuff when there wasn't any Brickwood's around, a good substitute like, with a punch like a kick from a dray-horse.

Lit-up and unsteady, Tubbs eventually left the boozer. Get back aboard unseen, especially by Brewster, was his aim. But he fell short of it.

He was sidetracked, waylaid, by one of those small boys with co-operative elder sisters. The small boy was nobody's fool. He knew very well that this drunken English sailor was much too far gone to appreciate his sister's services, but that was the English sailor's fault, not his. Overridingly, the small boy's interest lay in the fact that English sailors, drunken ones with golden badges, had much, much money. And in the insalubrious back alleys of Port Said there lurked dangerous men who would offer reward for the delivery of a gold-mine.

'How far offsh your shister, mate?'

'She is not far. She is very, very cheap. She is very beautiful, very large tits. You come with me, I show.'

Tubbs had no idea where he was being led, but he knew *what* was leading him and wouldn't be denied. He was all for it; lucky he'd met the little bugger. Off they went, deep into the dark alleys and the stench of drains, of ordure in the road, of hurrying figures wrapped in filthy clothing, with knives not wholly concealed. Tubbs didn't really register all of this.

A little after one bell in the first dogwatch, Petty Officer Brewster approached Lieutenant Newman and saluted.

'First Lieutenant, sir. Beg pardon, sir. Leading Seaman Tubbs, sir, not returned aboard. From a dental appointment, sir.'

'What time was the appointment, PO?'

'In the forenoon, sir. Due back by noon, sir.'

'Ah.'

Brewster hissed a little. Bloody Jimmy, didn't know what to say, what to do. 'It's now 1635, sir.'

'Yes. What do you suggest, PO?'

As he'd thought, couldn't cope on his own. 'Well, sir. Wait for 'im, I reckon. Then slam 'im int' report like. Adrift over leave, sir, which is what 'e is.'

'All right, PO. Thank you.'

'And likely returning aboard having drink taken, sir.'

'Drink taken?'

Oh, my God. 'Drunk, sir. Boozed.' Petty Officer Brewster

rose and fell testily on the balls of his feet. 'What constitutes another crime, sir. Another charge.'

'Yes, of course. Thank you, PO,' Newman said again, and Brewster saluted, turned about and marched away. Stone the crows, some people, some officers, they were still wet behind the ears.

Newman looked after the PO with a frown forming. He'd heard stories about Port Said. Not nice stories. And Tubbs, it seemed, was well adrift by now; and he wasn't the sort to risk his rate and his good conduct badges. Not willingly. Newman decided this was a matter for the CO.

'I should damn well think so,' Tom said. 'Thank God you reported it. Brewster should have shown some sense, and reported much earlier.' Tom had many experiences of seaports, especially those on the South American run – Recife, Rio de Janeiro, Montevideo, Valparaiso. 'Anything could have happened,' he said, 'it's certainly not like Tubbs. Is Lasenby aboard?'

Newman said he was.

'Tell him to go ashore – at once. Inform the naval police – the Provost Marshal. The patrols'll have to make a search. I don't like this, Newman. Get cracking at once, old man, all right?'

Tubbs had set a problem; not an unusual one, but serious. Port Said covered a large area of insalubriousness and vice. Sailors sometimes didn't have much sense. The search would take time and Tubbs might not have much left. The bad boys didn't hang around once they'd got their hands on a victim. And it was seldom possible to pin the many crimes on to the perpetrators – they covered their tracks with wicked efficiency.

The patrols, however, were vigilant and thorough even if they were too late. By midnight a body had been found, stark naked, with a number of stab wounds and a cut throat. The body was white and bore tattoos on both forearms. A twisting snake, a heart pierced with an arrow, and an anchor.

It had been found in an open sewer on the outskirts of the town. A report was made at once to the *Geelong*. Tom was called to make an identification; he recognized Leading Seaman Tubbs.

When the word reached the lower deck, the reaction was general: shame it wasn't Brewster. Wardroom opinion was the same.

FIFTEEN

THE TRAGEDY CAST A GLOOM OVER THE whole ship. Tubbs had been a popular man, a leading hand who'd been able to maintain discipline without ever being a bastard. Also, his death was an operational loss: he'd been a first-rate gunner. In Port Said, replacements were not easily come by. Tom made a report to the staff at naval HQ ashore; he included Tubbs' personal details as shown in his parchment, the linen-based document that accompanied each rating throughout his service career, going with him from ship to ship. Tubbs had been married with two children, lived in Devonport. The naval staff would do the necessary, informing Tubbs' port division at RN barracks, who would inform the wife. In the meantime, Tom knew it would be expected of him to write less formally to the little family.

'What on earth do I say?' he asked Frank Newman. 'How can I put it?' The facts would have to remain forever hidden from the wife and children. Tom had an idea that all such letters included something about the man giving his life bravely for his country . . . that sort of thing, whether or not it accorded with the facts. 'Met with an accident while ashore' might cover this case. But perhaps a widow's pension might be affected if the man was not in the performance of his duty. A visit to the dentist, on orders from the ship's doctor, as Tom had already told the staff ashore . . . a man had a duty to maintain his health for the sake of the ship's efficiency, and teeth were a part of health.

Tom gave a heavy sigh as he began the difficult letter. An accident while ashore on duty . . . no need to mention that

Tubbs had been adrift over leave and thus technically on a charge.

When a man died on duty in wartime, or in peace-time come to that, the naval custom was to hold a mess-deck auction of his personal gear for the benefit of his dependants. At these times a lot of generosity was shown, articles going for many times their value. Already such auctions had been held aboard *Geelong* in the cases of the men lost in the recent action. Now it was Tubbs' turn.

The bidding was high, reflecting Tubbs' popularity. Tom made a donation of five pounds: the wardroom officers collected a similar sum. Petty Officer Brewster watched the proceedings with a sour face. He knew that his own demise would produce little enough.

'Load o' flannel,' he said when approached for a donation, having not bid at the auction. 'Brought it on 'imself, didn't 'e? Whoring around in a dump like Port Said, oughter 'ave known better.'

'He's still pegged it,' Petty Officer Popplewell said. 'Doesn't matter how, does it?'

Brewster breathed out heavily, down his nose. He said reluctantly, 'Well, death's death, like.' He raked in his pocket and came up with a florin. British – you couldn't spend it in bloody Egypt. 'That do?'

Two days later, the *Geelong* was ready for sea. They all knew the ship wouldn't be left in port for longer than was necessary and there was no surprise when Tom returned from a summons to naval HQ with his sailing orders. He spoke privately to the officers in the wardroom. The hint that had been dropped to him earlier, the hint that he had half conveyed to Grant-Wylie in the bar of Shepheard's Hotel in Cairo, had been confirmed.

'We sail at 1300 tomorrow, after taking bunkers,' he said. 'Destination UK.'

There was a buzz of comment. Grant-Wylie's face lifted into a grin of sheer delight and relief. Mr Wenstock looked enigmatic: home but no wife, not too good. Tom went on, 'We'll call in at Gibraltar if necessary to take on more bunkers. After that, it's Ireland. Haulbowline, in Cork. Whilst we're there, we're to be fitted out to take concealed depth-charges – an extra punch against the U-boats – and further strengthening throughout the ship to take another 4.7 amidships.'

Mr Wenstock said, 'That's going to mean a longish job of reconstruction. A full due in port.'

Tom agreed. 'Yes. The ship'll be turned over to the dockyard. And since it'll be in a home port, my guess is that we'll be dispersed, paid off. But so far that has not been said. If it does happen – well, I'll be sorry to split up, but I suppose that's the way it goes. In the meantime, we prepare for coaling at first light tomorrow morning. From then on, it's back to tramp-ship rig.'

And the war, the everlasting watchkeeping and the lookout for the U-boats.

Secrecy had yet to be maintained – so far as humanly possible. Nothing of their destination would be revealed to the lower deck until the ship had passed de Lesseps outward bound. But the lower deck always had an uncanny instinct for arriving at the truth. Within half an hour of Tom's wardroom talk, the buzz had spread: they were going home. There would be home leave, port and starboard watches taking their turn. Right away, their thoughts turned homeward and plans were being made. There were the usual jokes about the married men.

'What's the *second* thing you do when you get home?'

'Take me boots orf.'

Able Seaman Barrett could hardly believe his luck. The missus . . . well, she'd be overjoyed, naturally. That apart, though, it wasn't so happy. It would be far from the usual home-coming, what with the lad in jug. He'd meet old shipmates in the Pompey pubs, and what was their reaction to him going to be? Standoffish? What the lad had done rubbed off in so many ways, tainted things. And whatever his boy had done, he wouldn't want to hear him pulled to pieces by his mates . . .

Very early next morning, the *Geelong* shifted to the coaling wharf and the detested business began once again. Tons of Welsh coal from the Rhondda brought in from the colliers out of Barry and Swansea and Cardiff, loaded into baskets, hoisted aboard and poured down the chutes into the bunkers to feed the boilers. A job for all hands, no one excused, and coal-dust penetrating everywhere, every body aperture, every chink throughout the ship – mess-decks and cabins, bridge superstructure, galley and heads, everywhere would be black and sticky and generally filthy, and a nightmare of a job afterwards, cleaning ship with the wash-deck hoses, the stewards' dusters a-flap around the cabins, and the scrubbing-brushes out along the mess-decks and ratings' accommodation. To Petty Officer Brewster, a buffer's torment. But tormented buffers had a recourse: they could torment others. Always a silver lining.

When the first of the baskets were coming aboard, and the lower deck had been cleared, Brewster went around on a snoop that he called a check that all ports and such had been closed against the swirling coal-dust and that everything that could be stowed away had been stowed away.

Like a crusher, a regulating petty officer of the ship's police, his feet trod the decks and his gaze penetrated every nook and cranny, seeking out slackness better known as being bloody idle. His very nose seemed to quiver like that of a bloodhound.

Ah! Two lockers improperly secured. He'd have someone's guts for garters over that, he would. He pounced. Idle, untidy sods. He attacked the first of the offending lockers, shoving at the contents and leaving the lid wide open so that plenty of coal-dust would get at the innards. That would show them, getting their personal possessions mucked up, photographs of the missus and kids and all. He took a note of the offender's name so that he could be put in the rattle. Then he rummaged in the next of the two lockers: Able Seaman Barrett's, what a piece of luck.

Rummaging, he struck gold.

A cutting from the Portsmouth *Evening News*. The name Barrett mentioned. Brewster read avidly.

A bloody conchie, a gaolbird.

Strewth!

At 1245 Tom climbed to the bridge. Below, Mr Wenstock stood on the starting-platform, watching the telegraph from the bridge. On the fo'c'sle and poop the hands stood by ready to cast off the ropes and wires leading to the shore bollards. Frank Newman, First Lieutenant, made his final report to the Captain.

'All hands aboard, sir, ship ready to proceed.'

No saluting now – back, as Brewster would say, to Whack. 'Thank you, Number One.' Tom cupped his hands to shout fore and aft, to Brewster and Popplewell in charge of their parts of ship: 'Let go headrope, let go sternrope.' Then to the Officer of the Watch, Sub-Lieutenant Lasenby in a trilby hat with a stained ribbon and a coal-dust-streaked vest: 'Stand by main engine.'

'Stand by main engine, sir.' The handle of the telegraph went over; bells rang on the bridge and in the engine-room. As the springs were cast off and brought inboard, Tom put his engine to slow astern, and the *Geelong* backed off the wall and turned for the main exit channel. At 1300 precisely the ship headed outwards to move into the Mediterranean. As they came past de Lesseps Tom put the telegraph to full ahead. Catching Newman's eye he said, 'I suppose they all know the score – that we're going home – but you may as well make it official now, Number One.'

Newman did so. Even though they all knew it by that curious galley-wireless magic, a cheer went up. It was left to Brewster to apply the damper – he disliked happiness. 'All right, all right, all right! You'll soon be drafted foreign again, the lot of you, don't you forget that, the war's not over yet, only just bloody begun.' He glared at Barrett. 'I s'pose *you*'ll be glad to be 'ome an' all. Or will you – eh?'

Barrett felt like murder. He knew Brewster had been at his locker and could hardly have failed to spot that cutting. Meanwhile the PO had asked him a question. Not to answer would lead to a charge of dumb insolence. Barrett wouldn't take any chances now of mucking up his leave entitlement back in the UK.

'Lost yer fuckin' tongue, 'ave you?'

'No, PO. And yes – I'll be glad to be home.'

'Oh, yes? In that case, watch it, Able Seaman Barrett.'

Barrett knew that Brewster was holding back on his sneakily gained knowledge, waiting to slam him with it, though God alone knew how, rotten bastard.

The weather was mild for the time of year as the *Geelong* headed through the Mediterranean. It was almost like summer, with a flat blue sea under a blue sky. A warming sun shone. The off-watch hands made the most of it, keeping on the open deck and avoiding the fug below. The weather might not last; it could turn quickly in the winter, though it was now verging on spring. Tom kept largely to the bridge; at any moment a periscope might be spotted and, as ever, speed of reaction was the key to salvation. While fully alert, his mind roved over many things, among them what his future might hold so long as the war lasted. He had achieved command through other men's misfortune; but it was likely to be only temporary. When the *Geelong* had been handed over to the dockyard authorities at Haulbowline Island, he would be without a ship, available for reappointment elsewhere. It was possible he might be retained to stand by the ship, but if so it was not likely he would still be in command when she sailed again with her newly fitted depth-charge racks. He had far from enough RNR seniority for permanent command. He could be sent anywhere at the whim of the Admiralty – another Q ship, a cruiser, a battleship . . . if the latter, then in all probability he would spend his time swinging round a buoy in Scapa Flow, growing idle in much comfort, communing with the sheep when going ashore, sheep being virtually the only inhabitants of that bleak, storm-swept place.

He thought about Grace Handley. Would she make contact again – would *he*? He didn't know his mind. He thought of the deanery that had been his home; he thought of his father, going steadily more senile. From Haulbowline he could go by train up to Galway easily enough, but the prospect was a depressing one. The Dean had been a gloomy man even in the good times.

His thoughts returned to the ship. He thought about Barrett, of what awaited him when he got leave to Portsmouth. A sad case, that. And he'd noted that Petty Officer Brewster had been getting at Barrett all along. That would need to be watched; but they hadn't much longer to go now. Eight days to Gibraltar, another five to the Fastnet and Cork harbour. Time for things to develop even so. But possibly the thought of home leave might mellow even a man like Brewster. Possibly.

The weather held. It began to feel like a summer cruise in peace-time. They passed units of the fleet, armoured cruisers and light cruisers from Malta, steaming east for the Suez Canal, probably under orders for the Indian Ocean, where German commerce raiders were known to be operating. The *Geelong* did not dip her ensign in salute as was customary between HM ships; such activity might be noted by a lurking U-boat commander and interpreted: the Q ships were already not as anonymous as once they had been. The Germans had been caught out too often, and had ticked over. But signals were exchanged between the *Geelong* and the flagship's signal bridge: Had an enemy presence been sighted in the Eastern Mediterranean? Such a question was normal; no suspicions would be aroused beneath the sea. Tom's answer was no. Friendly messages were also exchanged: *Bon voyage*, and good luck.

Two days after this encounter the bridge watch raised the Rock of Gibraltar. They came round Europa Point and continued past Gibraltar Bay and Algeciras, heading for Cape Trafalgar and Cape St Vincent and into the Atlantic. Mr Wenstock had reported coal enough in his bunkers, and no need to call in at Gibraltar.

Once into the Atlantic they met a change of weather. They steamed into a heavy sea; the temperature dropped, the barometer fell back fast. Tom took all precautions for a blow. The Blake slips and bottle-screw slips on the anchor cables were given an extra turn and heavy stoppers were passed as a further precaution. The seaboat's falls were overhauled, the gripes tightened. Deadlights were screwed down hard over the ports; lifelines were rigged along the open decks and along the tween-deck. In the galley and stewards' store-rooms, and in the cabins and mess-decks, everything movable was secured so far as possible. Below decks there was an unpleasant cold fug. There was no cheer anywhere.

'One thing,' Brewster remarked. 'It's not U-boat weather. The sods'll not come near the surface in this. Makes us nice and safe. We hope.'

He turned round. Barrett was securing a lifeline. Brewster said, 'Make a good job of it, all right? Don't want no nasty accidents, do we?'

'No, PO.'

'And take that surly look off of your face, Able Seaman Barrett. What's up with you, eh? Thoughts of going home, is it, what you'll be faced with in Pompey?'

Barrett flushed, hands letting go of the lifeline, balling into fists. Holding on to his temper he said nothing. Brewster's lips thinned. He said harshly, 'Going home to a bloody conchie, lad what leaves others to do 'is fighting for 'im. Ought to be bloody put before a firing squad if you ask me.'

Barrett lost all control. He lashed out with a heavy fist, taking Brewster on the point of the jaw. Brewster went down on the wet deck, tried to get up and lost his balance. As the ship rolled heavily to starboard, he slid willy-nilly towards the guardrail, arms and legs scrabbling at the deck. The tilt of the ship carried him beneath the guardrail, and he went overboard in a helpless, screaming heap.

SIXTEEN

TOM WAS ON THE BRIDGE. HIS REACTION was immediate. 'Stop engines! Away seaboat's crew.' He cupped his hands and shouted for'ard, 'Lifebuoy in the water, pronto!'

He saw Barrett run for the guardrail and climb over. Well, he wasn't going to stop him. If Barrett was lost along with Brewster, it might be a happier end. The alternative, if Brewster couldn't be fished out, would be a charge of manslaughter, maybe murder. That, and Barrett's son. To die might be preferable.

The seaboat was quickly lowered and slipped, pulled round to face aft – with way still on the ship, the *Geelong* was leaving Brewster behind and Tom couldn't risk moving his engine astern; the danger from a revolving screw would be too great. Meanwhile Barrett was striking out towards Brewster, who seemed to be near his last gasp, just a white face and an upflung arm. Like so many of the old seamen, Tom thought, Brewster may never have learned to swim: death from a sinking ship came quicker and easier if you couldn't swim, maybe thousands of miles from land in shark-infested waters. But in the current circumstances Brewster would have been better off being able to keep afloat.

Barrett was drawing closer now. Tom watched in a kind of agony, willing Barrett to make it. The whole of this scenario was a horror for any commanding officer: a lower-deck fight, ending in drowning . . . Tom sent up a heartfelt prayer, a prayer for deliverance short of drowning from the evil that was Brewster. Knowing Barrett's trouble, knowing Brewster's hazing of the man, he was as certain as he could be that the PO had provoked the whole thing.

Then he saw Barrett reach out and grab Brewster into his arms. Lying back and floating, Barrett held Brewster fast on top of his body, hanging on for the seaboat's approach. Tom blew out a long breath of relief when he saw the boat's crew reach over and take hold of the two men.

When the seaboat had been hoisted on the falls and Barrett and Brewster helped out on to the deck, they were sent below for Grant-Wylie to check them out. They were both given tots of rum, wrapped in blankets, and sent to their bunks, not in fact much the worse for their experience. In forced accordance with naval discipline Barrett was segregated in a spare cabin with an armed sentry on the door. The charge against him was a serious one; in a ship equipped with cells, that was where he would have been locked.

Tom felt immense sympathy for him but there was little he could do. During the afternoon watch Barrett was brought formally before the Officer of the Watch to be charged, in the official wording, with 'an offence against good order and naval discipline in that he did strike Petty Officer Brewster his superior officer'. He was passed on to the First Lieutenant and then to the acting CO. Tom had him brought before him the following morning, the charge being laid by Petty Officer Popplewell. In the interval, Tom had mugged up a smattering of naval disciplinary law from King's Regulations and Admiralty Instructions.

'Have you anything to say, Barrett?'

'No, sir.' Barrett's face was set, obstinate. He didn't want to talk about conchies. 'No excuse, sir.'

The facts were known, but Tom was duty-bound to ask the question. 'Do you admit the charge?'

'Yes, sir.'

Tom studied his face. Brewster had already given his

testimony in a tone filled with venom. Able Seaman Barrett had struck him without provocation after being spoken to in terms of moderation about his work on the lifeline. His manner had been surly from the start . . . Brewster had obviously wanted to elaborate about Barrett's manner but Tom had stopped him. Nothing that had gone before was relevant to the present charge. Tom made the only pronouncement he believed possible. He said, 'Remanded.' This meant that no sentence would be passed until there had been full consideration by higher authority in the UK. Tom spoke to Barrett again: he would, he said, see him privately in his cabin later. Brewster began to object. Tom silenced him. 'That'll do, Petty Officer Brewster.'

'If you say so. Sir.'

Tom ignored the words and the tone. PO Popplewell took over. 'Remanded, on cap, salute the Captain, about turn, double march!' Barrett moved away under escort. Brewster was obviously seething. But he relieved his feelings in the petty officers' mess, which he shared with Popplewell, the Chief ERA and the stoker POs.

'Skipper don't know 'is fuckin' job . . . letting that article talk to 'im in private! Never 'eard the like. After what the bugger did. Any road,' he added with some satisfaction, ' 'e'll bloody face court martial when we gets to Haulbowline. Bloody hell! Striking a PO aboard ship in wartime.'

'Kind of asked for it, didn't you, eh – bringing up what you did about his kid?'

Brewster rounded on him. 'And you just shut your trap and all, Petty Officer Popplewell.'

Tom was plagued with doubts. He was unsure as to the whole fandango of the Naval Discipline Act. But on balance he believed he had done the only thing possible in the circumstances. Any commanding officer of Captain's rank or below was limited as to what punishment he could apply. Certain crimes had to be judged higher up the chain; certain punishments could be awarded similarly. Remand was the safest course; remand meant the charge and its consequences could be referred to a senior officer on arrival at Haulbowline. Tom's self-doubts were in fact concerned principally with the effect on the ship's discipline. There was going to be a lot of sympathy for Barrett, and a lot of contempt for Brewster – who had still to function effectively as the ship's senior NCO.

Tom had his private talk with Barrett.

'This is between you and me, Barrett. You can speak freely.'

'Yes . . . thank you, sir.'

Tom hesitated, looking Barrett in the eye. 'Have you had news from home recently? In Port Said. Anything you've not told me?'

'Well, sir.' Barrett stared at the bulkhead behind Tom.

'Go on. If you don't tell me, I can't help.'

'No, sir.' After another hesitation, Barrett told him. 'They're holding the lad in custody. Remanded, like, to Winchester Quarter Sessions. You know the charge, sir? Demonstrating outside the main gate o' the dockyard . . . assaulting a copper.' Barrett swallowed. 'The missus, sir . . . she sent me a cutting from the paper.'

'I'm very sorry,' Tom said. He was as helpless in the matter as Barrett himself. He said, 'Tell me more, Barrett. Tell me precisely why you struck Petty Officer Brewster. It wasn't just his attitude, was it? What else was there?'

'Personal matter, sir. Just personal.'

'I know that, it's obvious. Just tell me this: was it personal on account of your son?'

'Yes, sir. Yes, it was. That bugger . . . sorry, sir, spoke out o' turn like.'

'Don't worry about that. I told you, this is private. But by "that bugger" I'm going to assume you meant Petty Officer Brewster – and you needn't answer that.'

A sheepish grin began to spread over Barrett's face. Tom grinned in reply. 'Right, point taken. So what happened?'

Barrett came out with it. 'That – Petty Officer Brewster, sir. When we was coaling in Port Said. Rummaged in me locker, the mess-deck being empty, sir. Found the cutting.'

'And taunted you with it?'

'That's right, sir. Said the lad should be put before a firing squad, sir.'

'I see. Barrett . . . if I'd been you, I think I would have done what you did. Now, I'm duty-bound to put the matter before the Commodore at Haulbowline. You understand?'

Barrett nodded. 'Yes, sir.'

'But I'll be doing what I can. It may not be very much. But I'll be putting in a word and they may listen. They ought to.'

They bloody well ought to. Tom had been shaken by what Barrett had said. Brewster was not fit to hold his rate, and it would be a wicked injustice if Barrett was to suffer. But suffer he would almost certainly have to: in the eyes of the Royal Navy there was never, positively never, any excuse whatsoever for striking a superior officer. Discipline had to be upheld, a petty officer's authority had to be upheld; but petty officers worthy of their rate didn't rummage around in other men's private possessions. It was despicable.

But what could be done about it – about Brewster? Tom's talk with Barrett had been off the record and, though he absolutely believed what the man had said, he would presumably have no actual proof that the rummager had been Brewster. If only he had, Tom thought in a sudden rush of fury, he'd have had a mind to run Brewster in on a charge of attempted theft . . .

As matters were, Brewster had to be suffered. Whatever happened, the ship's efficiency, her safety as she neared home waters, must in no way be prejudiced. Brewster had to be treated in the normal way.

That night the weather worsened considerably. As the

Geelong left Cape Finisterre on her starboard quarter and came into the Bay of Biscay she met storm force winds, winds that gusted to around a hundred miles an hour, buffeting the old ship with their formidable strength, piling up towering waves that swept the decks from fo'c'sle to poop, swilling around the well-decks fore and aft so that the poop, bridge superstructure and fo'c'sle stood out like islands in an inmensity of rushing turbulence. During the middle watch the engine-room voice-pipe reported three stokers injured, one with a leg broken after being flung across the greasy metal deck of the boiler-room, two with severe burns after falling against the red-hot mouths of the furnaces. Grant-Wylie was roused out from his bunk to go below, where he organized stretchers to bring the stokers up to the tween-deck.

Tom kept to the bridge while his ship laboured. He had difficulty in keeping his feet as the deck lurched and heaved to the confused swell of the Bay. It seemed not so far off Cape Horn conditions, days when often enough four helmsmen were needed on the wheel, all of them securely lashed for their own safety, and the mate on watch hanging on grim-faced to wherever he could find a handhold. By now the order had gone out that all hands were to keep off the upper deck; even with the lifelines, the conditions were too dangerous. This meant that the watchkeepers stayed where they were, no reliefs, watch-on stop-on until the weather moderated. The cold was icy; the bridge personnel remained soaked through to the skin.

It was at seven bells in the morning watch that Petty Officer Brewster, standing by the gunport doors with a party of seamen dealing with leaks around the seals, gave a scream of agony and fell to the deck, writhing around and clutching his gut. Five minutes later the voice-pipe whined on the bridge: Grant-Wylie, speaking from the wardroom.

'Petty Officer Brewster . . . developed peritonitis. I'll have to operate at once.' The doctor's tone conveyed the urgency. 'Can you hold the ship at all steady?'

Tom's answer was immediate. 'Not a chance. You'll just have to carry on – and good luck.'

Brewster was brought to the wardroom, which was hastily rigged as a makeshift operating theatre. Still screaming out obscenities, the PO was laid on the wardroom table. Grant-Wylie was assisted by his SBA and the wardroom steward: Brewster might need to be held down. Grant-Wylie applied the ether mask, and Brewster quietened. When he was unconscious, Grant-Wylie made his incision. He was, he said afterwards, only just in time. Brewster's face was as white as chalk; and there was a lot of blood and pus. Brewster's beer gut was not easy to cut through. But the diseased appendix came out in the end, to be dropped from Grant-Wylie's forceps into a jamjar containing formalin. 'A get-home present for his wife,' Grant-Wylie said.

When Brewster had been tidied up and bandaged, the doctor spoke to the bridge, wiping sweat from his forehead. The motion of the ship had been hell, the wardroom table rising and falling as he probed into Brewster's stomach, making the operation potentially lethal. 'All over,' he reported.

'Will he live?'

'He'll live,' Grant-Wylie said. 'I'll report again when he's come round from the anaesthetic.'

Tom banged the voice-pipe cover shut. Brewster seemed to be a natural survivor. First the fall overboard, now this. It wasn't fair; Tom conscientiously stifled further unworthy thoughts. But, however unlikely, it was to transpire that a miracle had taken place that stormy night.

Soon after a late dawn the weather moderated a little. The glass rose, as did the temperature; the wind lost some of its weight. The signs were good for a fair-weather landfall in due course. Grant-Wylie reported again at two bells in the forenoon watch: Brewster had come round. More or less; in fact he'd been out for longer than Grant-Wylie would have thought likely. And the coming-round process was not yet complete.

'What's his state, then?' Tom asked.

'Wuzzy. Not co-ordinating. Vomiting. Nothing serious – I think – but it's rather strange. He's wandering.'

'In what way?'

'Well – mental. Load of talk. Effing this and effing that, and references to God.' Grant-Wylie paused. 'And something about seeing things. A vision.'

'What sort of vision, for heaven's sake?'

'That remains unclear. But there's something on his mind . . . that's all I can say.'

'What are you going to do about him, Doc?'

'Put him in his bunk and keep watch. I'll report again when things clarify.'

Tom grunted. He had little sympathy for Brewster. 'What sort of state's the wardroom in?'

'Messy. Blood and pus. The stewards are coping, but if I were you I'd not come down for breakfast yet.'

Tom paced the bridge. He was dead tired, and he was hungry. He wanted to make port now, make it in safety. So many landward concerns to be sorted out.

Two days later, in fair weather with a stiff breeze and a wintry sun, the masthead lookout reported land. 'On the port bow, sir. The Fastnet.'

There was no relaxation yet. Never, until you'd made port. The U-boats could be anywhere.

'Dunno, sir. Funny like. In a white dress, giving like a sermon, nearest I can say. Blokes with wings . . . girls too. Could be angels I reckon. Come at me sudden.'

This was to the doctor. Brewster put it differently when Petty Officer Popplewell looked in. 'Never bloody credit it you wouldn't, not in a three-year bloody commission up the soddin' Yangtze. All lit up . . . white light . . . end of a bloody great tunnel. An' this old bloke at the end, behind a table. Like the skipper at Defaulters.' Brewster looked immensely puzzled. 'Kind sort of bloke, though, not pusser RN.'

'What d'you reckon, then?'

'Reckon it was God.'

Popplewell was right out of his depth. He'd had an aunt who used to do weird things, table-turning and that, and she dressed in a purple cloak for what she called communion with the spirit world, but that was as far as it went with Popplewell. He asked, 'What did this old bloke want with you, then?'

'Still trying to work that out, like. Fuckin' weird really. Sorry. Shouldn't 'ave said that.'

'Said what?'

'Fuckin'.'

Popplewell scratched his head. 'Never known you to apologize for swearing, mate.'

'Things is different now.'

'It sounds as though his brain's been affected,' Tom said. 'Is that likely medically?'

'No. At least, I've never yet heard of an appendix having any effect on the brain. I can't explain it whichever way you look at it.'

'Misspent life? Some sort of wish to atone?'

Grant-Wylie shrugged. 'Unlikely, but you never know. Maybe the effect of anaesthesia – but don't quote me on that, because I really have no basis . . . I just don't know.' He frowned in thought. 'All I can say is, he's got something on his mind as a result of . . . well . . .'

'Of what?'

Grant-Wylie grinned. 'Seeing God, I suppose. And the angels. Mustn't forget them. His wife came into it too. He said he recognized one of the angels as his wife.'

Tom looked up sharply. 'Some sort of – what is it – thought transference? Or a forewarning that his wife's dead, something of that sort?'

Grant-Wylie just didn't know, had no helpful theories to offer. He excused himself. Busy, he said; not just Brewster, there were the stokers. And at last a case of VD, caught in Port Said. Just the one man didn't constitute a CDA mess, but he'd have to be segregated.

One more worry for a commanding officer.

SEVENTEEN

THE *GEELONG* WAS NOT FAR OFF THE Irish coast and was beginning her approach to Cork harbour and Haulbowline Island when the leading telegraphist reported a signal from C-in-C Western Approaches. The orders for Haulbowline were cancelled; the ship was to proceed to Devonport dockyard. Tom went into the chart-room and laid off a course for Plymouth Sound.

Newman, Officer of the Watch, said, 'I wonder what's in the Admiralty's mind now, sir? Second thoughts about depth-charges?'

Tom shrugged. 'Who knows – and I'll bet the Admiralty doesn't!' He paused, thoughtfully. 'Could be the Home Rule boys, creating trouble.'

'The Fenians?'

'Sinn Feiners, yes. The Fenians are farther back in history.'

Newman remembered Tom came from the west of Ireland. 'Any trouble around your way, sir?'

'Connaught's a very Home Rule part of the country. If things get really nasty . . .' He said no more; he hoped there would be no riots, no shootings to upset his father. The Dean was a staunch King's man, had never had any time for the Republican cause or the wild men who supported it with guns and bombs, such as had already been used against British troops in Dublin. Unhappy events were taking place in Ireland, another bloody chapter in Ireland's long story of violence. Oliver Cromwell, still very much alive in Irish hearts and minds, had much to answer for. Tom had seen the iron ring-bolts to which Cromwell's army had tethered their horses in the aisles of St James' Collegiate Church in Galway City, the church being used as a stable by the Ironsides.

Tom pushed Ireland out of his mind for the moment: there were the other worries coming up. That early evening, the *Geelong* made her approach to the port of Plymouth, coming between the Eddystone Light and Rame Head. Passing through the breakwater she headed across the Sound, turning to port into the main entry channel for the dockyard, coming past Drake's Island and leaving Plymouth Hoe to starboard, that cliff-top patch where Sir Francis Drake had played the game of bowls that had gone down in history. Proceeding slowly through the Hamoaze, the ship received her berthing signal from the King's Harbour Master. Coming alongside a little later, Tom watched from the bridge as the ropes and wires went out to the shoreside bollards; and when Petty Officer Popplewell, standing in as buffer in Brewster's place, reported all secure, he passed the final order.

'Finished with engines.'

Below, after a quick check round, Mr Wenstock left the starting-platform and went to his cabin, misery tearing at his guts. What a home-coming, eh? No wife, an empty house waiting in Pompey. Nothing would be the same now. All the things they'd done together . . . but better not dwell on all of that. He wasn't the only widower and he just had to get on with it as best he could.

Next morning a naval ambulance came alongside and Petty Officer Brewster was taken off, to be conveyed to the Royal Naval Hospital at Stonehouse, where he would be for probably the next ten days. According to Grant-Wylie's SBA, who took news of him to the mess-desk, he was still on about God and the angels, still convinced he'd seen them. He hadn't sworn since he'd come fully round from the anaesthetic . . .

*

Tom was in his best monkey-jacket, all ready to go ashore to make his reports to the office of the Commander-in-Chief Plymouth, including a submission on behalf of Able Seaman Barrett as promised, when he was called to the shore telephone situated on the dock. The caller was an assistant surgeon from Stonehouse. He had charge, under the fleet surgeon, of Petty Officer Brewster. And Brewster wished to see his commanding officer.

'What's it about?' Tom asked.

'Hard to say . . . he's not very coherent. But he seems to regard it as urgent.'

'Is his life in danger?'

'No, no – he's mending nicely, it's not that. It's his mind. I'd really be grateful if you'd drop by soonest possible.'

Bugger Brewster. But he was a mentally sick man, it seemed, and C-in-C's office could wait a little longer. Despicable as Brewster might be in what he had done, he was still one of Tom's responsibilities. He said he would come right away. He telephoned for a taxi.

Brewster was half sitting up in his bed. His face was as white as a sheet and his hands were trembling, plucking at the blankets.

'It's the wife, sir.'

'Yes, Brewster?'

'Got a letter, sir. Me sister-in-law . . . the missus stayed with 'er after 'er ma's funeral. In Leeds. Same thing happened as with her ma, run over like. Not a bus, though – brewer's dray. Squashed flat, sir.' Tears were pouring down Brewster's face. 'Never appreciated 'er proper, sir, I didn't. Kep' 'er short o' money for one thing. Now the Lord 'as told me like not to be mean. Wish I hadn't bin. And 'er death's me own fault. You may ask why, sir. Reason is I was *glad* when 'er fu— 'er ma copped it. It's the vengeance o' the Lord, who told me plain when I see him after me appendix came out. Told me I'd bin a sod like, though 'e didn't use that word I have to say, but I got his drift all right. And 'e passed a warning like.'

Brewster went on and on. That angel he'd seen, the one who'd looked like the missus. She really had been the missus, up there already. (The brewer's dray had done its work a few days before Brewster's appendix.) The Lord had been very firm that he must change his ways and not be a so-and-so any more.

That was the gist of it; but Brewster had something more to say. 'That Barrett, sir. What I did, well, I reckon it could have like rubbed off on the wife, via God. Could have bin responsible. So what I'm asking is this: drop the charges, sir.'

'Drop the charges?'

'Yes, sir. That's my considered wish, sir. Get me off God's Defaulters like. Least I can do, sir.'

You didn't look a gift-horse in the mouth. Tom asked Brewster once again if he was certain in his mind that he didn't want the charge to go ahead. Brewster was positive. Tom reminded him that once the charge had been formally dropped, he couldn't go back on his decision. Brewster was adamant; and looked much relieved at having got it off his chest. There would be joy in Heaven; there always was, over a repentant sinner.

Tom left the ward with good news for Barrett and with no need to bother the Commander-in-Chief's staff with a serious offence.

Grant-Wylie had telephoned the pregnant girl as soon as he got ashore. All was well; and she was overjoyed to hear him, to know he was back. He had other news to report: that morning, a copy of the latest CW List, the list of officers' appointments, had come aboard with official papers from C-in-C's office. Grant-Wylie was to take up an appointment at RNH Haslar near Portsmouth in fourteen days' time. 'I'll get leave meanwhile,' he said. 'We'll fix the date as soon as possible.'

She said Mummy would be much relieved in the circumstances. Grant-Wylie was slightly nettled at that immediate response. He wasn't too concerned about Mummy . . .

Leave was given to the watches before the *Geelong* was taken over by the dockyard. Thereafter the ratings would report to their port divisions for draft to other ships or establishments. Able Seaman Barrett, a free man, took the train to Pompey, dreading his home-coming as much as Mr Wenstock if for different reasons. The case had not yet been heard by the quarter sessions. The boy would still be in custody; Barrett would perhaps be allowed to visit. If so, that would be a painful interview, a sad reunion rather than a happy one. The first sight of home, when Barrett took the tram from Portsmouth Town station, was shattering if not unexpected. The windows fronting the little street were all boarded up. Bricks. And no point in paying the glaziers to repair what would at once be smashed again. His wife was in tears, held him as though she would never let him go. On one of the boarded-up window spaces someone had been busy with red paint. COWARDY COWARDY CUSTARD.

Tom stood by the ship during the leave period. Four days after their arrival, a letter came from Grace Handley. She had contacts in Portsmouth dockyard to which her husband had been attached and she knew the *Geelong* was in Plymouth. It so happened (really?) that she had intended visiting Plymouth for a little holiday. She would be staying at the Grand on Plymouth Hoe, arriving in two days' time. If he cared to call.

He thought about it. He decided it would do no harm. After her scheduled arrival he telephoned.

'Grace?'

'Tom.' Her tone spoke the words she didn't say. She wanted him badly; a hint of tears. Tears of joy. They met in the lounge that evening, sat together looking out over the darkening water of Plymouth Sound. Ships passed, inward and outward bound. The war went on.

'Will it ever end, love?'

'One day it'll have to.'

Banalities. A kind of constriction. They both had a lot to say, but couldn't say it. There was a kind of caution in Tom that told him that he mustn't dig, mustn't precipitate anything. Mustn't let either of them commit themselves. He could see the way the wind was blowing. She wanted marriage; he was not yet ready, for her or anybody else. Not while the war lasted, anyway. Soon he would leave the *Geelong*. He would be given leave, probably fourteen days during which he would go across to Ireland and see his father for what could so easily prove to be the last time. And after that?

Reappointment – to anywhere in the widespread British Empire. Hong Kong, West Indies, Singapore, Australia . . . and the seas between.

Grace put a hand on his arm. They sat very close, not speaking. It was as though she had sensed his thoughts, those thoughts that were projecting ahead over war-torn seas. And then they heard, faintly at first then louder, the skirl of the pipes and the drumbeats of a highland regiment marching in the dusk along the Hoe. They moved to the big windows. The pipes and drums of the 42nd Regiment – the Royal Highland Regiment, The Black Watch. Tom recognized the tune, one commemorating the time when, a century before, a battalion of the regiment had been on active service in Africa, fighting the Ashantis, and had been left virtually forgotten by the War Office for no less than twenty years during which time they had been under-supplied and were literally in rags and tatters. The march epitomized their eventual trooping home to the Broomielaw in Glasgow; Tom had mostly forgotten the words but recalled something about 'kiltie cauld-bums' and 'bare-arsed buggers' marching down the Broomielaw.

He murmured the words. Grace gave her remembered giggle. 'Where are they going, Tom?'

'Probably about to embark aboard a trooper. Farewell parade . . . foreign service, maybe France. The front line.'

'Oh . . .' She seemed to catch her breath. Then the pipes and drums shifted, merging into 'Auld Lang Syne' . . . *'Though seas between us braid hae roar'd, Since auld lang syne . . .'*

'Oh love, don't you go away too.' She held his arm very tight, and, looking down as the pipes receded into the distance towards the Citadel, he saw the tears run.